Thetis, crying bitterly to her son Achilles:

"*Alas! Oh my son, Why did I bear you and raise you only for misfortune? You should have stayed by your ship without tears and laments, for your destiny draws near and your life is to be far too short. Today, of all the men in the world, you are both the one who must die the soonest and the most sorrowfully. Since the day you were born in my palace that has been your unfortunate fate. Nonetheless, I shall go to the snowy peaks of Olympus to speak to Zeus, lightning-thrower, of your wish. Stay here for now, near your swift vessel, and nurse your anger. Guard your furor and cease to fight. For yesterday Zeus left over the ocean, to visit the Æthiopians and share a magnificent banquet. All the gods have accompanied him …*"'

Homer: *Iliad 1.413-24*

"Hold fast and hold back"
Anekhou kai apekhou
    Stoic's motto

THE ETERNAL BANQUET

Jennifer Macaire

Published by Accent Press Ltd 2019
Octavo House
West Bute Street
Cardiff
CF10 5LJ

www.accentpress.co.uk

ISBN 9781786154583
eISBN 9781786154552

Chapter One

The sky was a vast blue upside-down teacup over our heads. The sun beat upon the wooden deck of the dragon ship and reverberated off the waves in a million sharp diamond points. There was not a breath of wind; the sails drooped listlessly. The chickens gasped in their cages, beaks wide, yellow eyes dull. In the hold, sunlight sparkled off the dust surrounding us in a nimbus of golden heat. We lay without moving. Beneath linen sheets, prickly hay smelled like mown fields under a blazing sun. Waves slapped against the wooden hull of the ship, but the sound didn't cool us.

When the heat grew unbearable, we would go above deck, sluice ourselves with buckets of seawater, then come back and collapse in the shade. The deck was blistering hot, and our wet footprints evaporated immediately. Whoever went on deck was expected to throw water over the chickens and goats. The animals huddled in the shade, panting miserably. We were no better off. Everyone waited in silence for evening when, hopefully, we could row out of the dead calm.

We were off the coast of the Iberian Peninsula near the country that, in the future, would be known as Portugal. If I shaded my eyes, I could make out a thin black line of high cliffs on the horizon. Our boat captain, Phaleria, wanted to avoid them; treacherous currents made the lack of wind deadly. At night, we would try to row towards the Pillars of Hercules where the wind would surely be present.

I glanced through latticed windows and tried to judge the time. At least another four hours until sunset. I lay back and tried to sleep. I was tired; we had been rowing all night. But it was too hot to sleep. Instead, I let my mind wander. My thoughts were vague at first, darting here and there, not settling on any one thing. The present was too hot. The future was uncertain. Our voyage had started well, but if we didn't get out of these doldrums soon, we'd run out of fresh water.

Dying of thirst would be a new one for the man lying next to me in the hay. Alexander, also known as Alexander the Great, pushed a lock of sweat drenched hair off his forehead and, seeing me staring at him, gave a wry grin. So far, according to historians, he'd died of malaria, poison, cholera, alcoholism, and acute pancreatitis. Only he hadn't died. I'd saved him.

Born in the far future, I'd won a prestigious award and had been chosen to voyage back in time for a day to interview the one of the world's greatest conquerors. Alexander had mistaken me for Persephone, goddess of the dead, and kidnapped me. We fell in love, and I saved him when he lay dying in Babylon. The rest, as they say, is history.

I leave out much of the story, like the part where I grew up alone in an echoing mansion, raised by parents who despised me, or when I married a man who tortured me mentally and physically. My childhood crippled me emotionally. But it was nothing compared to Alexander's. Raised by a hysterical mother and a violent, alcoholic father – abused by his mother, beaten by his father – it's a wonder he became the leader he was. He credits Aristotle for helping him. I think he's partly right. He also says love saved him. My love, and Plexis's – Hephaestion's – love saved him, as well as the love of our children and friends. In the end, it all boils down to love.

We had left the British Isles after Demos and Phaleria celebrated their wedding. The sea was clement and the wind brisk. We made good time to the coast of Gaul where we docked near the mouth of the Seine River. On a rocky pier jutting out of a long, grey beach, we traded with a tribe of Gauls.

The dragon boat made a huge impact wherever we arrived. Most people hung back, waiting prudently to see who was sailing it. When they saw it wasn't raiders, they approached and traded with us, asking for the latest news and giving us news of their own. That's how we heard about Carthage attacking Tartessos.

Alexander grew agitated and asked a million questions. I was afraid he'd start to shake the fellow who was giving us the news, so I took him by the arm and drew him away.

'Alex, calm yourself. You're no longer responsible for Greece.'

'But that was one of our best trading posts. It was Phoenician, not Greek,' he said, running his hand through his hair, a gesture that meant he was upset.

'When you captured Tyre you conquered the Phoenicians,' I reminded him. 'In the history books it says that the Phoenicians "had a great civilization, which ended with the conquest of Alexander the Great".'

'They say what?' His hand froze, comically, on top of his head. His face showed a mixture of emotions, as usual. 'I never meant to *end* any civilization. I left them their government. I left them their trading posts, like Tartessos. I even let them keep on wearing their silly hats. I never ended anything.' He looked forlorn.

'Their silly hats?' I raised an eyebrow – a trick I'd learned from him.

He just shook his head. 'Carthage.' The word was said with a queer mixture of anger and longing. I knew what it was. He would have loved to have captured Carthage for his own.

I looked at the crowd standing on the pier. Demos was easily visible, a head taller than the other men around him. Near him was his new wife, Phaleria, her bright red hair plaited into two tight braids reaching her waist. She wore copper arm bracelets, a gold necklace, gold earrings, and silver rings. Her clothes were gaudily coloured and lavishly embroidered: a bright yellow skirt, a green tunic, a blue shawl, and a red vest. She looked every part the wealthy Celtic trader.

Nearby, listening to the gossip, was Nearchus. He had grown a curly beard and it made him look even more serious, if that was possible. He had been Alexander's admiral for ten years, and his smiles were as rare as summer snow. Right now, he looked grim. His loyalties lay with the Greeks and Phoenicians, not with Carthage.

Alexander's and my son, Paul, stood next to Yovanix, who had stopped wearing his bandage on his blind eyes, baring his scars to the world. They still made me shudder, for I had been the one to put his eyes out. Yovanix could always tell when I looked at him. He told me my glance was like a cool touch, and sure enough, he turned towards me and his handsome face lit up in a smile. Axiom, Alexander's valet, was on the dock as well.

As we stood near the boat, green waves crashing against the rocky shore, I noticed tall megaliths in the distance guarding the entrance to what looked like a grove of sacred oak. Wanting to get a closer look, I left our group and went to explore.

'Where are you off to?' Plexis, bored with the trading, joined me.

'I want a closer look at those stones.' I pointed, then lowered my arm, confused. 'They're not there any more.'

'What aren't there?'

'Big stones, standing in line in front of the trees.' I rubbed my eyes with my hand. Dazzled by the light? No, the sun was behind me. I was sure I'd seen megaliths. 'I'm going to have a look anyhow,' I said, and set off. There was a path leading to the woods. It was late summer and the air was full of pollen. Gold, scarlet, and blue flowers bloomed in the salt meadow where flocks of sheep grazed. Beneath an apple tree, I spied a young shepherd playing a tune on a wooden flute.

'Excuse me,' I said, addressing the shepherd in my awkward Celtic. 'Is that grove of trees sacred? Can I go to look?'

The youth put his flute down and stood. 'I'll take you. The grove *is* sacred, but everyone is welcome.' He had replied in Latin. I gave him a closer look. He had swarthy skin and black, shiny hair. His eyes were black as well, but when the sun hit them I saw they were dark purple, like mulberries. 'I've been expecting you,' he added.

Plexis stepped in front of me protectively. 'What do you mean? Who are you?'

'You can call me Myrddin.' He nodded towards the forest. 'And I've been expecting you because I'm a druid.'

There was a whisper of metal on leather as Plexis drew his sword from its sheath and pointed at the youth's throat. 'Don't move,' he ordered. To me he said, 'Call Alexander. I'll hold this one here. Hurry, we'll —'

'That's not necessary. I mean no harm, to you, Hephaestion, or to you, Ashley of the Sacred Sandals,' the shepherd said with a laugh.

I gaped at the boy. 'How did you know our names?'

'I'm Myrddin.' He shrugged. 'Come, you wanted to see the stones, didn't you? I'll be your guide.'

Plexis didn't lower his blade. '"I'm Myrddin" is not an explanation,' he said.

Myrddin looked startled, then closed his eyes and seemed to listen to a voice in his head. 'You will know me better as Merlin. I was waiting for you, Ashley, to explain

6

that we do not usually meddle in fate. What is written in your books *shall* come to pass. I'm sorry Voltarrix found you. He started a rebellion in our clan, and I am not yet strong enough to have been able to stop him. I want to assure you that the druids are your friends, not your enemies.'

A nervous laugh escaped me. 'You? Merlin the Enchanter? You're in the wrong time. Arthur won't be born for another three centuries.' I put my hand to my head. 'Did I fall off the boat and knock myself out?'

'No, you didn't fall, and yes, I know the future king won't be born for while. I will have to wait, but I won't be bored. According to the legends, I'm going to Albion to build Stonehenge.' He gave a rueful shrug. 'I can't help it, I see all the centuries at once, as if they were pages in a book. Sometimes I get confused.'

Plexis frowned at me. 'Do you believe him, Ashley?'

'I don't know what to believe. You do see him, don't you? A young man with black hair, talking about legends? He mentioned Albion but in the future, it's called Britain.'

'Yes, I see him too.' Plexis sighed and sheathed his sword. 'I don't suppose you're going to listen to me and go back to the boat now, are you?'

'Come.' Merlin turned and walked towards the grove of trees.

'You're not going to listen, *are* you? Can't you be reasonable for once?' Plexis asked me.

'I can be reasonable,' I admitted. 'But not this time.' I trotted after Merlin. After a moment, Plexis followed.

We stepped into the shade of the trees and followed a well-trodden path to a large clearing. Here, Merlin turned to face us. 'Hold my hands', he said. I'd scarcely touched his hand when it turned dark, as if a lid had slammed down on us. I opened my mouth, but Merlin said, 'Hush. Just watch.'

In the penumbra, I saw glimmers of light. A group of men entered the clearing in front of us. They paid us no heed. They carried rough torches made of burning branches. On their faces were streaks of coloured clay, and rough furs hung from their backs. They had dark brown, nearly black skin, and their blue eyes were pale in their faces. Black, curly hair covered their heads. They didn't speak, but growled and grunted. They paused in the middle of the clearing then became transparent and disappeared.

The darkness seemed to deepen. After a moment, a new group of men crowded into the clearing. They were dressed in rich clothing. Some had velvet capes and others wore silk doublets and lace collars. They carried swords, but one had a pistol. The group huddled together for a moment, and one man looked up at the sky and said, '*Ma bone espee que ai ceint al costet, tut en verrez le brant ensanglentet! Jo vos plevis!*' The others raised their fists and cried, '*Jo vos plevis!*' I knew they were swearing by the blades of their bloody swords, but the French was archaic. As we watched, they too, faded.

The glade became lighter, and a new group of five men, dressed in ancient army attire, stumbled in. I recognized them as being soldiers from the Second World War. One was wounded. They scanned the area and flinched, as if hearing sounds we could not. 'I'd sell my grandmother for a drink of water,' said the wounded man. He could barely stand. Two other men held him upright. 'Be quiet, Sean.' whispered a soldier. He hefted his rifle. 'How much ammunition do we have left?' Before anyone could answer, the group of soldiers disappeared.

The glade was empty except for a deer. Carefully, it moved across the clearing, looking for shoots to eat. It nibbled on a bramble bush, then a noise must have startled it. It raised its two heads and looked around. One head turned one way, the other head turned in the other direction. One head was fully formed but the other had no eyes; skin covered its eye sockets. It lowered the blind head and began to graze and then, like smoke, it vanished.

Merlin released my hand. The scene shifted. We still stood in the woods, but sunlight dappled the ground. Plexis gasped. 'What happened to that animal?'

'The deer? It's from all the radiation. After the great divide, we ...' I stopped. Plexis looked ill. 'I'm sorry. The scientists say it's getting better. In a few centuries, Europe will be liveable again.' I felt like crying and glared at Merlin.

'Time is a strange thing,' said Merlin. 'I didn't show you that to upset you. I wanted to show you how time is like a piece of mica. There are layers upon layers, and all are transparent. I can see through those layers. It is my gift and my curse.'

'What about the stones? I said. Did they ever exist?'

'Yes, they are over there, in the deep grass. They are lying down, but soon men will come and raise them.'

9

We went back into the meadow and sure enough, seven megaliths lay on their sides. They were freshly hewn. I could see the marks left by the chisels. Gouges in the stone glittered in the sunlight. I climbed on one and stood, balanced on the warm granite. Plexis climbed up next to me. 'We can see the shore from here,' he said.

'Yes, There's Alexander. He's waving at us. They must have finished trading.' I turned to Plexis. 'Do you want to talk about it?'

He shook his head. 'No. I told you once before, you've ruined the future for me. Perhaps there is something good in it, but I have yet to see it.'

Merlin shook his head. 'Ashley is a child of the future,' he chided. 'So there *is* good there too. She doesn't see things the way you do, Hephaestion. I hope you will remember my words. She acts without thinking of the consequences sometimes, but her heart always guides her. Follow her heart. You will be safe.' With that, he bade us farewell.

When I boarded the ship, I looked back at Merlin – or Myrddin, whoever he was – and waved. He raised his arm, the wind picked up, and we sailed out to sea. The water turned from blue to green. Plexis didn't speak to me for a whole day, but when he came to me, he opened his arms, inviting me in.

'I'm sorry,' he said.

I pressed my cheek to his chest. 'You were upset. I understand.'

'It was cruel to say you ruined the future. None of it is your fault. And Merlin was right. There *is* good there, if it produced you.'

Our next stop was further down the coast, to stock up on supplies. Paul and Plexis went into the village with Axiom to buy mineral water. This place was famous for its sacred springs. The waters here were supposed to cure rheumatism and various other ills. Axiom suffered from rheumatism in his elbow and wrist, which was not surprising; he'd broken it badly when he was a child and it hadn't been set right.

Paul and Plexis had also taken Paul's young dog Perilous with them. They were busy training it to be a guide dog for Yovanix. So far, they'd trained the dog to walk sedately and sit on command. Plexis trained horses, so he was confident he could train a dog.

Yovanix was standing near Demos. That day he wore a white linen bandage around his eyes. I turned my head, but not before Alexander saw my expression. 'It wasn't your fault,' he said softly.

'Everyone keeps telling me that., but it was my fault, even if I didn't know it was him. It's so unfair.' I rested my head on his shoulder. 'Why do I feel so close to you?' I asked. 'How is it that I want you to hold me in your arms and never let me go?'

'Never, ever let you go?' he asked, eyes hooded.

'Hold me forever,' I agreed.

'Because you are melancholy. I feel it too sometimes. Usse gives me a potion for it. But I will be your potion.' He smiled and kissed me. 'What happened in the land of your

11

ancestors was a terrible shock for you. You lost a hand and you nearly lost your life. You watched a terrible druid cut my throat, and you were barely able to save me.'

'Those were not the worst moments though,' I said, burying my face in his neck. 'When I had to kill those men, that was the worst.'

'It wasn't as if you'd never killed anyone before,' he said. 'Look what you did to poor Bagoas.'

'I can feel you giggling,' I said, my voice muffled. 'It's not funny. I didn't want to kill anyone.'

'Except Bagoas.'

I pulled back and looked at him. His face was still. Too still. I had the feeling he wanted to laugh. 'Why are you in such a good mood?' I asked.

'Because, I have my soul back. I feel whole once more. I spent a year with the feeling I would fly apart, that the wind could blow me away. I was lost in a cold maze, and you and Paul saved me. Now I am whole again, I'm with the people I love, and we are heading towards home. The sun is bright, the sea is sparkling, and the druid's potion against seasickness works wonders.'

'That's good.' I frowned. 'After the news you heard, are you still planning to visit Carthage?'

'Yes, why?'

'You better keep your opinions to yourself. I don't think they'll appreciate someone coming to their city and complaining about Tartessos.'

'I *never* complain', he said loftily. 'Do you see that gull? I bet I could bring him down with one arrow.'

I followed his pointing arm up towards a white speck, wheeling in the cerulean sky. Small cirrus clouds were wisps of cotton high above us. It was a perfect day. And Yovanix would never see it. He would never see anything ever again.

'Stop thinking sad thoughts,' ordered Alexander, taking my chin in his hand and turning my face to his.

'I'll try.'

'Yovanix has ceased to lament his misfortune. You will do well to do the same. He needs your cheerfulness, not your crying. He wants to feel part of our family. He doesn't want pity like a beggar on the street would get.'

'You're right, absolutely right. I'll try to remember.' I smiled suddenly. I couldn't help it. The sun was picking out all the metallic lights in Alexander's hair and making his parti-coloured eyes blaze. He had his jaguar stare again. He wore the supremely confident look of a man in the prime of his life.

'You're doing it again,' he said.

'What?'

'Tempting the gods. Stop looking at me like that. They are jealous. Temper your gaze and calm your heart. We will sacrifice a lamb tonight to Zeus and Athena; they will appease the others on our behalf.'

I heaved a sigh. 'You are being silly.' I turned away and stared out to sea. I didn't believe in the gods. Alexander didn't want to. Everyone else around us believed. They would appreciate the sacrifice; a tasty grilled lamb would make a nice change from fish, fish, and more fish.

'Ashley, Ashley of the Sacred Sandals turn and look at me. Cast your frosty eyes in my direction and quench the thirst in my heart. Let me touch your marble-smooth skin and run my hands through your pale, silken hair.' His voice was low and teasing, his breath hot on the back of my neck. I tried not to grin, but his eyes, tiger sharp, saw my mouth twitch. 'O Queen of Ice and Darkness, come here, I have something to show you. Shall we take a little walk? I know of a quiet stream to bathe in. Will you come with me, Ashley of the Arrow Miracle?'

'Now that you've used all my titles, how can I resist?' I said, good humour restored. 'Shall I use all of yours?'

'No, we'll be here until sunset if you do. Just say Alexander of Alexandria, that should cover a few places.'

'A few? That makes ten I know of. And that's only here and now. In three thousand years there will be at least three times that number, scattered all over the world.'

'How flattering,' he said, trying for modesty. But modesty was not one of his expressions. Although he had all the others, and then some, modesty would forever elude him.

I followed him to a shady brook where we bathed in sweet, cool water. The stream was clear amber, flowing over slippery round pebbles the size of my fist. Small trout darted in and out of the dappled light. Overhead were the huge, spreading branches of sacred oak trees. A sandy beach dipped into the water. Around it bloomed profusions of late summer wildflowers: yellow buttercups, purple digitalis, white nettles, and blue larkspur.

'How did you know this was here?' I asked, wading into the hip-deep water, stepping carefully on the slick stones.

'I asked.' He grinned. 'Do you like it?'

I watched as he lifted his tunic over his head, baring a muscular torso. 'Mmm, I like it very much,' I said with a wink.

He lifted an elegant eyebrow. 'I hope so, it's been ...' he paused, '... a while.'

The longing in his voice found an answering throb in the my body. We met midstream. A willow tree cast sweeping branches over a deep pool in the bend. Alexander held me around the waist with one hand and parted the lacy, leafy curtain with the other, and we ducked through. Inside the cover of green, I felt as if we were in an enchanted place far away from the rest of the world. Under the tree, in the green, dappled light, the only sounds we heard were the willow leaves whispering softly.

Alexander splayed his hands against my ribcage, then cupped my breasts. His breath came fast. When he touched them, a tiny moan escaped him. His eyes were hooded with longing. We didn't speak. Our bodies spoke for us. Our arms and legs recited poetry to each other; each touch was a promise, each caress a fulfilment.

I closed my eyes and traced the line of his body with my right hand. I felt each sinew and muscle, each tendon and scar. I knew the shape and feel of his bones, and they were precious to me. My left hand was no longer part of me, but the inside of my wrist and arm were sensitive. I felt his heart pounding.

There was a mossy bank behind us. I don't remember how we got there. I think Alexander lifted me onto it. One minute we were in the water, then next I was lying on soft moss. All I knew was that I needed him, in me, that minute. The weeks at sea with no privacy had kept us apart. No longer. I wrapped my arms and legs around him and guided him into me.

We held each other tightly, coming together with limbs that trembled and a chorus of soft moans. I abandoned myself to the rise and fall of his body. It *had* been a while. Excitement submerged us, we were helpless in its grip. It was over far too quickly. Afterwards, he leaned his forehead against my shoulder. Our skin was damp with sweat and heat. The sunlight filtering through the branches of the willow coloured our bodies green. I felt like Alexander was the river god and I was his nymph locked in his embrace.

Alexander lifted his head from my shoulder and said, 'You have ruined me for anyone else.'

'Is that bad?' I asked him, my voice shaky.

'No, I don't think so.' He stepped back into the water and helped me down off the bank. He smiled crookedly. 'It's not a bad thing. But it makes me want to live a life of peace and quiet with you and our children.'

'Near the banks of a river,' I said blandly.

'In a tent with a beautiful rug and with a glass lamp swinging gently in the breeze.'

'With a gold and ivory writing set, an ebony table, and a jade bowl.' My voice was suddenly very soft. A keen melancholy washed through me and I recognized it for what it was for. 'Is it possible to be homesick for a tent?' I asked.

'We spent ten years in that tent. It was our home. But we'll never be able to live that way again. Perhaps that is why I need you so. You anchor me to my past; you make my memories come alive. With you, I can imagine myself in Persia again under the tall date palm trees, watching the white, curly-haired goats grazing in the shade. When my arms go around you, I feel my youth return. You are everything that's sweet and good in my life. With you, there was nothing but victory and joy.'

'And loss and terrible sadness.' I whispered.

'I even love remembering our loss. Because my memory of Mary is part of you. It is something we share and binds us together. Like our children are proof we both exist.' Tears were running down his face. He wore his emotions on the outside, like most people of that time. He cried easily and laughed easily. After more than ten years, I was starting to show my emotions also.

I brushed the tears off his cheeks. 'You exist. Never fear. And you will continue to exist long after the dust of your bones has been dispersed by the wind. Three thousand years, through the ages, be they dark or golden, your legend will still shine. It will be a beacon for some, a mystery for others, a tantalizing myth for many. And it will stir the heart of a girl born into a cold world of indifference and pretence. It will save my life.'

'I kidnapped you from Hades.'

'That's exactly what you did,' I said, kissing his mouth, taking his bottom lip in my teeth and biting it gently. 'Hold me, Alex, hold me. Sometimes I think of the things that could have gone wrong and I can hardly breathe. Then I thank all the gods I've ever heard of that you were strong enough to tear me free of the tractor-beam.'

'Oh, that was nothing. The hard part was getting used to your accent afterwards, when you lost the gift of tongues.'

'It's called a tradi-scope, and it was disconnected after twenty hours.'

'Your accent is much better now. You don't sound like a bad actor playing a Mesopotamian whore speaking Greek.'

'That's a relief.'

'And your Celt is coming along nicely.'

'We've been here for a year. Oh, Alex, I miss Chiron and Cleopatra so much. When will we arrive back home?'

'Soon, Ashley, soon.'

'The problem with you is that soon can mean three months, while for me soon means five minutes.'

'Your world had no notion of time?' His eyes twinkled.

After we left, we headed out to sea intending to stay away from the coast of Iberia where fierce tribes lived in the swamps and river land. We would trade with the Celtiberians in the south after we passed the Pillars of Hercules – the strait of Gibraltar.

But then we'd hit a patch of glassy sea, and we'd been becalmed ever since.

I fanned myself and lifted a lock of hair from my neck. Sweat ran down my chest and forehead and beaded on my upper lip.

Sweat shone on the bodies of the men lying near me, making their skin gleam like gladiators. Phaleria's face was almost as red as her hair, and her green eyes looked like bright emeralds in her flushed face. She leaned on her elbow and peered out the lattice window. 'I think we lost a chicken,' she said.

'We'll have him for dinner,' said Erati, the boat's chef.

'We won't have to cook him,' said Plexis, without moving. 'It's so hot, he'll be well roasted.'

'We can fry the eggs on the deck, no need to light your oven tonight,' said Vix.

'Who said anything about lighting my oven? Just the thought makes me ill.' Erati got up and groaned. 'I'm going to take a swim.'

'Erati?' Phaleria said.

'Yes?'

'Watch out for the sharks.'

'If one bites me he'll burn his mouth,' said Erati. He ducked through the low door and trotted quickly across the deck and tossed the rope over the side while he danced on the hot wood and hauled up a bucket of seawater. In truth, no one had any intention of swimming in the sea where black fins surged out of the deep water, and flat, round eyes stared at us above mouths full of jagged teeth. I'd rarely seen so many sharks. Instead, Erati took the bucket and tipped it over his head, letting the water cascade over his body. With an audible 'hiss' it hit the deck and I saw steam rising off the wood. The chickens ruffled their feathers when Erati splashed water over them and the goats shook like dogs. He took more water and sluiced it over the deck, cooling it off the best he could. Then he dumped another bucket of water over his head.

By the time he came back to his place he was practically dry. The heat was intense. Phaleria raised her eyebrow at me, and I nodded. Going from the shade into the sun was like entering an oven. I gasped and winced as my feet hit the wooden deck. It was so hot it felt cold at first, then it burned.

We took turns pouring water over one another, then sluiced the deck again because it was already dry. I checked the chickens, but they seemed to be alive. Hot, but alive. I reached through the slats of their pen and poked at an egg.

'What do you think?' I asked Phaleria.

She sprinkled water over the goats. 'Soft boiled,' she said, 'I'm sure.'

We ran back to our shelter. It was quiet. Alexander was sitting, trying to capture some breeze. Nearchus seemed to suffer the least. He was reading, a scroll on his lap, a serious expression – as always – on his noble face.

Yovanix was playing a game of chess with Axiom. His deft hands picked over the pieces he'd carved, deciding which move to make. To distinguish the black pieces from the white ones he'd carved tiny scales on them. Now, with just a light touch, he could tell which were which. He often beat Axiom, no small feat.

Plexis and Paul had both fallen asleep. Paul was snoring lightly. He had his father's proud nose – and soft snores. Plexis lay on his back, arms outspread. His dark hair was damp and curled with sweat, his mouth slightly open. I saw Alexander's gaze linger on his friend and lover, his eyes softening. But the heat kept us all well away from each other. To touch was to burn. We fanned ourselves with folded papyrus and sweltered.

In the shade near the doorway, Oppi, one of Phaleria's crewmembers repaired a torn net. After watching him tying the knots, I asked him when he'd started sailing.

'Not long ago. I was a barbarian from the Black Forest, but the tall trees gave me claustrophobia,' he told me, in his rough voice. 'I always wanted to see the ocean. It invigorates me. I also wanted to travel,' he said, putting the net down and spreading his hands. 'Why spend all your life in one place when the whole world exists? Why does it exist, except to be seen?'

'Or to be conquered,' I said, tweaking a curl on my husband's head.

Alexander turned his head towards me and smiled. 'To see, to conquer. Why not?'

I laughed. 'Someone will say something close to that. He's going to say, '*Veni, vidi, vici*; I came, I saw, I conquered.' He'll be Roman.'

'A Roman *would* say that,' said Plexis, waking up and yawning. 'Or maybe Iskander here.' He grinned, dodged a kick, then sneezed. 'This hay is nice, but dusty,' he said.

Demos stretched, taking up most of the room, and then sat up, picking hay out of his hair. 'By Helios, it's hot. Look, the sun's touching the horizon. Soon the air will be cooler.'

He had started to grow a beard as well, but it was growing in rather patchy because of the many scars on his face. He scratched his whiskers, tipping his chin up. His

21

broad chest was covered with thick curls, as were his arms and legs.

Alexander, having been raised Greek, shaved his beard. He also shaved his chest, though I begged him not to.

'But I'll look like a barbarian,' he'd exclaimed.

The men in Gaul had beards or moustaches. They wore their long hair in braids and had hair all over their bodies, which made Alexander reminisce about his first wife, a barbarian named Barsine.

I had truly liked Barsine, a jolly, red-haired barbarian princess who had borne Alexander a son and had died from complications. It seemed to me impossible that someone as strong and energetic as Barsine could have succumbed to childbirth. It made me sad to think about her. As Alexander often said, there was only one Barsine. He, too, grew quiet when he thought of her. However, I think it was also because he missed their son, Heracles, who lived with his grandparents in the Zagreb Mountains along with the rest of his massive tribe. Alexander had seen him but once, and he'd given the orders to Artabazus, the boy's grandfather, to hide him if he ever heard of Alexander's death. He hadn't wanted the boy to become part of the bloody struggle for his empire, and so Heracles had disappeared into the fog of history.

We hoped he was living happily with his family, high in their mountain retreat. As far as my history books had taught me, the boy had never been found. He wasn't on the casualty list that had included: Olympias, Alexander's mother; Roxanne, Alexander's fourth wife; and her ten-year old son, named Alexander. Dead also were Craterus and

Lysimachus, two of Alexander's generals; Stateira, Alexander's second wife; and Iollas, his cupbearer.

Stateira had perished first when she made the fatal mistake of announcing her pregnancy to Roxanne, who poisoned her. Poor, foolish Stateira, she'd trusted Roxanne and hated me. It was true I was jealous of every second Alexander spent with her – horribly jealous. But I would *never* have poisoned her.

Iollas was next. He was a twelve-year old boy, son of Antipatros, one of Alexander's oldest and most trusted generals. Olympias, in her folly and sorrow, accused Iollas of poisoning Alexander and had the child strangled.

Sisygambis, Darius's mother, would starve herself to death, dying a mere five days after Alexander's body was found.

Behind us, in Babylon, nothing was left but ashes. Black robes and ashes, and the civil war, which had been going on for three years. Roxanne's son was three years old. He had seven more years to live.

The thought made me cold, even in the sweltering heat of the cabin. I shivered, an icy trickle of sweat running down my back. I hadn't told anyone about this part of the future. It was too awful. Luckily, Alexander was outside with Plexis, dumping buckets of water over their heads. Plexis would have known my thoughts. He somehow picked emotions out of the air. He was with Alexander and in the blinding sparkle of the sun, their bodies shimmered like mirages. Taking a step forward, Alexander took Plexis by the hand and drew him into a quick embrace.

No one blinked, except Nearchus, who closed his eyes for a moment. He would always love Alexander, but he knew Alexander only admired him. I lowered my gaze before Nearchus caught me watching him. I knew what it felt like to watch the person you love caress someone else. I was lucky – Alexander had never loved his other wives, he only loved me – and Plexis.

In those days, physical contact between men was considered as normal as that between men and women, possibly more normal in some societies. Women were mostly equated with the three 'C's: childbirth, chores, and chattel. Friendship only existed between men, as did love. Paradoxically, pure homosexuality was frowned upon. Men were expected to marry and raise children, but they were expected to love other men. Go figure. Most of the time, the closest ties existed between men friends, rarely between men and wives.

Women lived in the gynaeceum, raised their children, wove their wool, and ordered their servants around. A gentle but tedious existence.

In Gaul, from what I could see, the sexes were equal; the women wore pants like the men, and marriages were monogamous. Only the men could be leaders, soldiers, or druids, but Yovanix told me women were often healers and could attend – though not speak in – council meetings in the villages.

The Celts were also a monogamous people. The women in Celtic tribes had more power than any other women of that time. I had seen many affectionate gestures between husband and wife, and also between men and between women. The Celtiberians were a savage tribe who loved to make war. Their men joined the army for life and lived together with a partner like the Thracians.

What was normal? I had no idea. I think that the world was still young and malleable at that time, and easily accepting of everyone's lifestyles.

We started rowing as soon as it was cooler. If we didn't make shore soon, our water supply would run out. That night, after five days of maddening heat and becalmed seas, we reached choppy water and a breeze came from the mainland to greet us. When dawn poked her rosy fingers above the horizon, we stood on deck and breathed deeply, the wind lifting the hair off our shoulders and putting a sparkle in our eyes. The chickens relaxed and went back to scratching in their hay and clucking, and the goats bleated contentedly as they butted their heads against the slats of their cages. Alexander was seasick again but, as he said, smiling wanly, at least he wasn't dying of the heat any more.

The current carried us towards the Mediterranean at a fast clip because the Atlantic Ocean was less salty than the inland sea. On the surface, the fresher, ocean water was drawn into the Mediterranean, while deep currents carried the saltier seawater out to the ocean. The result was a heavy chop with the boat being carried along like a cork.

Chapter Two

We reached the Pillars of Hercules early the following day. In good spirits, we hoisted the sails higher and sailed along the coast. The Mediterranean was only five kilometres across from Europe to Africa at that point. We were on the European side. Phaleria wanted to trade for pewter before heading across to Africa and Carthage.

The villages of the Celtiberian tribes along the coast were independent. They were ruled by chieftains. Later, perhaps in fifty or a hundred years, Carthage would conquer the Iberian coast and wipe out or enslave most of the villages. Carthage wanted to control the silver and pewter mines the Iberians had exploited since the dawn of time. Rome would then defeat Carthage, and the Iberians would be absorbed into the immense Roman Empire, their culture gone forever.

This was an opportunity to study the Iberian civilization first-hand, I thought to myself, as we tied the boat to a huge iron ring set into a stone dock. The time-travel journalist part of me was thrilled. I wished – for the millionth time – that I had a holo-cam with me to record everything, but I'd have to make do with my diary, which I tucked into my bag and carried everywhere. Everyone at that time had a diary –

some were amazing. Plexis was a talented artist, and Nearchus, though he spoke little, was a captivating writer.

We arrived at a pleasant-looking place with cultivated land reaching up the mountain's flank and a fortified citadel on the hillside. After we left the fishing village, we took a wide sandy road through groves of almond and fruit trees up the hill towards the city. We walked slowly, savouring air that was warm and fragrant with the scents of peaches, almonds, and woodsmoke. We were hoping to find rooms in a comfortable inn. We were heartily tired of sharing the same cramped space, sleeping on linen-covered hay, and washing with salt water.

Along the road, women carried clay water jugs on their heads as they returned from their evening trip to the wells, with children tagging at their heels. The sky was deep violet, the sun had set and the only shadows were cast by torches planted every twenty metres or so along the white sand road. In the dusk, tree trunks looked ghostly. Shepherds gathered around small fires and the scent of cooking meat wafted to us, making our mouths water.

The road followed the natural curve of the land, rounding the base of a hill then climbing steadily in a spiral. The sprawling citadel, built right at the very top, was further than it had first seemed, and to get to it we had to cross a long bridge spanning a deep chasm.

Alexander examined everything with the interest of a born conqueror, judging the width and depth of the chasm, the height of the walls, and the best way to attack.

'I like the idea of the wall there, it looks haphazard, but it's not. See how the road curves sharply? An army trying

27

to sneak up on the city will be obliged to group tightly to get past that bend, and then you've got them.' Alexander sounded wistful. 'The defenders can shower them with spears. The attackers would be helpless unless they adopted the rectangular shield I perfected. Remember, Plexis?' His voice brightened.

Plexis looked at him over his shoulder and flashed a grin. In the dark, his teeth gleamed. 'With the rectangular shields held over their heads they could protect themselves from above and the wall would become a liability instead of an advantage for the defenders.'

'Be quiet, you two,' I said, taking Alexander by the hand. 'We're tourists, remember?'

'Tourists?' Alexander looked surprised and then grinned. 'I forgot, as usual. So, tell me what you know about this place, Ashley. What will become of it? Will it resist the forces of time? Or will it too turn to dust and the mountain free its shoulders of its stone trappings?'

'It will become a city called Malaga, I believe. It won't be built in the same spot, but it will be nearby. The vineyards will remain, the port as well. It will prosper. Its geographical placement lends itself to a logistical necessity, a link between the mountains and the inland tribes and trade. It will become a chic tourist resort, and in my time, it is a cultural centre for holo-ship voyages.

'I forgot how pedantic you could be,' Plexis sighed, turning to peer at me. 'And how frighteningly cold you sound sometimes. I still get the chills when I remember what you said about Babylon.' He was teasing me, a sparkle in his amber eyes.

'I think it's interesting,' said Paul, linking his arm through mine. 'Tell me more, Mother. Wasn't it "Spain" on the map you made me?'

I nodded, content with my son. I gave lessons to Paul in the evenings; 'future' lessons as opposed to history lessons, using a map I'd painstakingly drawn of the modern world. Axiom took care of the history, and Alexander tutored him in maths and science. Plexis taught him riding, fencing, and Greek; Demos taught him cuneiform writing and Persian; Phaleria gave him lectures on trading and the geography of the coast and Gaul; and Nearchus taught him navigation and astronomy. Everything a ten-year-old should study in that time. When he got back to Alexandria, Paul would take up his lessons with his tutor and add epic poetry, the classics, religion, Egyptian, and Latin.

I insisted on teaching him Latin, much to Alexander's amusement.

'Latin? No one speaks Latin. Teach him Greek, or Phoenician. Everyone speaks those languages.'

'Not for long,' I said. 'It will be good if he learns Latin, then he can teach his own sons.'

'Yes, but your accent is strange. At least let's hire a real Roman and let him do the job correctly.'

'Good idea; we'll take care of that when we reach Rome,' I said.

'Yes, we can buy a slave,' said Alexander, giving a wink. He knew how I felt about that.

'Very funny. Are we almost there? I'm starving, I'm tired, and I want a bath.'

We entered the city through a large archway made with flat slabs of rock. It was like a tunnel, and we stopped speaking as we walked through its blackness. When we reached the other side, I uttered a sigh of relief. I hated the feeling of being hemmed in. A legacy of spending one year in a stone prison.

The dark tunnel led directly onto the main street where torches burned brightly, lighting the way for us. The sandy road underfoot changed to cobblestone, with raised wooden sidewalks lining the road on either side. Very Celtic. We strolled along the main street, admiring the two and three-storey houses made of stone, brick, and wood. The windows were large, with wooden shutters to keep out the sun and ventilation holes along the tops to let air in during the long, hot days. Balconies made of forged iron were fixed on the second storeys and held up with wooden beams. Woman set their looms on them during the cooler part of the days, and at night families sat there and watched the crowds below.

The prosperous city was crowded, full of traders from all over: Greeks; Phoenicians; Egyptians; Gauls; Romans; and Celts. The Celtiberians distinguished themselves from their neighbours by the way they dressed. The men wore vests over their bare chests, and tied large, colourful belts around their waists to hold up their pants, whereas the Gauls tended to wear suspenders and undershirts.

The Celtiberian warriors were also fond of putting chalk and water in their hair and then letting it dry into fantastic shapes: huge points, curving horns like bull's horns, and spikes all over their heads. Very odd. I tried not to stare.

Our innkeeper greeted us warmly. He bowed, as was the custom, and welcomed us with a bowl of olives and pewter tankards of cool water. He wore his dark hair in braids, like most Celts, and he shaved his beard but had a drooping black moustache. His eyes were very black and his skin was pale. A true Celtiberian. Their skin would become darker when the Moors crossed the Straits of Gibraltar and took control of the peninsula for a brief time. He put a linen towel over his arm and showed us to a free table, telling us that dinner that night was roast goat with olive sauce, fresh fish, pickles, a salad of almonds and peaches, hard cheese made from sheep's milk, with wine or water to drink.

Dinner was delicious. We ate sitting on a bench at a long, wooden table. We watched the rest of the customers, listened to their conversations but spoke very little ourselves. We were tired, and the boisterous crowd, after the silence of the ocean, made our heads spin.

Afterwards, we made our way to the baths; a stone building set up near the village well. The brick bathhouse was built in a circle. Stone arches held a roof supported by wooden beams and covered in clay tiles. Women and men didn't bathe together. Every four hours the heated pool was emptied and a new group could wash. Before Phaleria and I could go to bathe, we had to wait until the men had finished. Meanwhile, we joined the line of women waiting to enter the baths.

The baths were heated Roman-style. A separate building housed a fire, and the heat was channelled through pipes under the round bathhouse. The water was about waist deep, and a bench ran around the entire pool, so people could sit and chat. There was some lye soap and shampoo, but I had my own from Gaul that I hoarded preciously.

After Phaleria and I had bathed, we floated in the warm water. I lay in the water, my hair floating around me, my arms and legs loose and wonderfully relaxed. Through the arches, I could see the night sky. Stars appeared like bright sparkles of diamonds in black velvet, their éclat unrivalled by electric lights.

Although people strolling by couldn't see into the baths, I could see flickering torches and the tops of the taller people's heads. The baths were Roman in architecture, a sure sign of their encroachment. But baths like this were still a rarity. The innkeeper spoke of them as if they were the eighth wonder of the world. People didn't take them for granted yet. And they were expensive enough to be available to only a certain class of people, unlike the public baths in Greece and Rome, which were free to their citizens – tourists had to pay, and slaves weren't admitted into the baths anywhere.

A bell rang, signalling time to change the water. We had to leave. I sighed regretfully and stood up, squeezing the water out of my hair. Phaleria admired the bump my belly had started to make. I was now four months pregnant.

She was longing to have a baby but, so far, three months had gone by and each time she'd been disappointed. I told her not to worry and to let time take its course. I also told her to stand on her head the next time she made love. Well, it couldn't hurt. We dressed and went to join our men, who had been waiting for us near the fountain. Afterwards, we strolled through the city, watching glass-workers ply their trade, admiring the pewter wares set out for sale, and listening to various street musicians, gossip, and newscasters.

The newscasters usually stood on a raised platform and held a scroll in their hands. When you dropped a coin in the basket – or hat – at their feet, they obliged you by reading the daily – or weekly or monthly – news. Usually well informed, these men started with the day's trading costs, giving the exchange rates, and telling which merchants were selling what wares. Then they moved on to the news about the town and the surrounding countryside, and then gave the news about the rest of the known world.

We found a newscaster and paid him, gathering around him to listen to the news. The man cleared his throat in an important manner and started reading from his long scroll.

'Excuse me,' said Nearchus, raising his hand, 'but could you speak in Greek?' Nearchus spoke a little Celt, but not enough for the news. And Celtiberians had their own dialect.

The man raised his beautifully plucked eyebrows. 'Greek traders?' he asked us. For simplicity's sake, we nodded. 'Fine. *Ahem.* Today, goat and sheep prices are stable, but olive oil has gone up. It's now two Greek obols for an amphora of olive oil sealed with pine resin. The mayor of the city has decreed a freeze on the price of bread, any baker charging more than —'

'Excuse me.' It was Phaleria. 'Could you skip to the part about pewter? I want to know how much that is trading for this week.'

'Fine, fine.' The little man shuffled his scroll, looking for pewter. 'Aha, here it is. Pewter is trading at eight ingots of pewter for one of bronze, seven ingots of pewter for one half of silver, and a Greek obol is stable at six for a drachma, which, as everyone knows, is quite a handful.' The newscaster stopped and chuckled at his own joke, then cleared his throat again. 'In the local news, someone broke into the wine cellar at the —'

'Pardon me, but could you omit the local news? Unless it's vitally important,' said Alexander, leaning forward. 'What news have you from Carthage? Or from Greece, or Alexandria?'

The man huffed in annoyance and shuffled down his scroll some more, looking for the international news. 'First, from Greece ...' He paused to see if we were going to interrupt again, but we stared up at him, polite interest on our faces. 'Aristotle is dead —'

'The monkey was right,' interrupted Alexander, 'Remember?' he grabbed my arm. 'The monkey told me — '

'Excuse me!' The man bent over and stared at us. 'What do you mean, 'the monkey told you?' When did you hear that?'

'He died nearly three months ago, I heard it from ...' Alexander's voice trailed off, and he frowned. '"A monkey told me" doesn't sound right, does it?' he whispered to me.

'Now you know what I feel like most of the time,' I whispered back.

'But, but ...' The news speaker was at loss for words. 'I only just *received* that news. It *just* arrived.'

34

'Hold on,' said Plexis, stepping forward. 'I haven't heard yet. When did it happen? How? You could have told me,' he said to Alexander. He sounded angry.

Demos tapped Alexander on the shoulder. 'Was it that monkey who could write? The one that told my fortune?'

Plexis gaped at Demos, then at Alexander. 'A monkey who could write told you Aristotle died?' he asked.

'I'll tell you about it later,' said Alexander.

'No! I mean, please, could you tell him now? I'd kind of like to hear about that too, if you don't mind,' said the newsman.

'Just get on with the news,' said Alexander, folding his arms across his chest.

The newscaster looked undecided, then shrugged and frowned at his scroll. 'So much for the big news of the day,' he muttered. 'Now, let's see. More about Greece. The war between Cassander and Olympias still rages, although it is mostly confined to the north of Macedonia. The Athenians have refused to participate, sending no soldiers to either side. The Spartans have sided with Cassander. For now, Antipatros still rules Greece, but swears he'll kill Olympias himself to avenge his youngest son, Iollas.'

'You can stop with the Greek news,' said Alexander, looking depressed. Iollas had been his cupbearer, and he'd been fond of the young lad.

'Fine, fine.' The man shook his head and muttered, 'Do they want the news or not? *Ahem.* So, let's get the scoop on Carthage, shall we? You heard about the attack on the Greek trading post of Tartessos? Yes? So, you know all the news about Carthage. The king of Tartessos was killed, by the way, and a noble from Carthage has taken his place. There is to be an important ceremony in Carthage to thank the gods in three weeks, at the rising of the new moon.

'Now for Alexandria near Egypt. Ptolemy Lagos has officially declared himself a god, so he is considered by everyone the official ruler of Egypt. We all bow down to him.' The man broke off and sketched a quick bow. 'And, for the very latest news from that kingdom, Ptolemy's son, also called Ptolemy, has been officially betrothed to the fair Cleopatra, the daughter of the late Alexander, King of All the World. *Hey!* What happened to her?' he cried, pointing with his scroll.

Everyone looked at the ground where I'd collapsed. My knees had simply given out at the mention of my daughter, Cleopatra.

It was not a faint, it was just the shock. The newscaster hopped off his pedestal, fanned me with a piece of papyrus, and said, 'I've never had *that* reaction before, amazing.'

'It's all right,' I said, sitting up and clutching Alexander around the neck with my good hand. 'I should have expected that, Ptolemy is nothing if not perfectly ruthless and ambitious. *Damn him.* Now I'll have to hurry back to Memphis, and I did so want to see Pompeii before the volcano annihilates it.' The shock was making me babble, I think.

'That won't happen for another three centuries,' said Paul, proud to show off his 'future' lessons.

The newscaster stopped fanning me and stared, his mouth hanging open. 'Well, I'll be,' he said. 'An oracle. I should have known.'

'I'm not really an oracle,' I said. I looked up at Alexander and sighed. 'I suppose that piece of information about Cleopatra doesn't bother you?'

'No. Think about it.' Alexander kissed me on the tip of my nose. 'It is good news. It tells us two things: first, Cleopatra is still alive and, second, she is under Ptolemy's protection. We can take our time. No one will dare harm our daughter.'

'You're delirious,' said the newscaster, nodding at Alexander. 'I said Cleopatra, the daughter of the great Alexander. He died in Babylon.'

'He was supposed to,' I said with a wince, getting to my feet and then leaning over, bracing my forearms on my knees while my head spun. 'Oh, I feel sick. It's a lucky thing that dinner we ate was good,' I said.

'Why?'

'Because I think I'm about to see it again,' I said weakly.

'Oh, no, you're not,' said Alexander, hoisting me upright and pressing a small vial to my lips. The strong mint drops calmed my stomach immediately. The druid had something there, I thought.

'Thank you. I'm feeling much better,' I said, my eyes tearing from the potion. '*Whew*, that's strong!'

Alexander beamed. 'It works wonders,' he said, 'I don't get half as seasick on those infernal boats as I used to. Amazing, isn't it? If I'd had this before, I would have conquered Africa, or gone to India by boat and conquered it from there.'

'You mean, the only reason we walked was because you get seasick?' Nearchus sounded upset.

'No, no! Of course not,' Alexander hastened to reassure him. 'We had to follow Paul.'

'That's true, we followed Paul,' said Axiom, his eyes twinkling 'Halfway around the world.'

'Well, at least you could follow something, because you've certainly lost me,' said the newscaster. He climbed back up onto his pedestal then leaned over to get a good look at us. 'You are the most confusing group of people to listen to. You,' he said, pointing to Alexander, 'Are certainly from Macedonia, and you,' this time he pointed to Paul. 'You speak a strange mixture of Persian and Greek. The redheaded woman is Celt, from Britain. Iceni, if I'm not mistaken. The large man is Persian. You are Greek,' he continued, pointing to Nearchus. 'Born in Crete. I'm never wrong about accents. And you sir, are certainly from Greece.' Axiom nodded, impressed. 'I am an expert on tongues, as are most of us newscasters and translators. But you,' he pointed to me, 'have the most bizarre accent. Almost as if —'

'Not another word,' I interrupted, holding my hand up. 'I know what I sound like, and believe me, I can't help it.'

'You should hear her speak Latin,' said Demos, a grin on his face.

'Oh?' The newscaster looked intrigued. 'At any rate, it's the first time I've been unable to identify an accent, so be fair and tell me where you're from.'

'All right,' I shrugged, it wouldn't make any difference. 'I'm from America.'

There was a silence as everyone around me digested this titbit of information. I'd never told anyone where I was from. Finally, the newscaster said, meditatively, 'America must be somewhere north of the Po valley.' But he didn't sound convinced.

We thanked him for the news and went back to our inn. For the villagers, the night was just getting started, but our feet dragged and our shoulders slumped. The thought of sleeping in a real bed in a real bedroom was enticing.

The bed was dirty and had fleas. The room was tiny, and the noise from the street kept me awake. Every time I'd start to slide towards sleep, a loud laugh, a shriek, or a barking dog would startle me awake. With a muffled groan, I buried my head under Alexander's arm and tried to ignore the fleas biting my leg. When, I couldn't stand it any more, I slapped at them, forgetting I didn't have a left hand. It's very frustrating not being able to scratch.

My head was aching when I woke the next day. Paul and Plexis had gone, and the bed was empty as well. Alexander always woke up at first light, no matter what. He was probably downstairs or at the baths. After a sweaty, flea-filled night, the thought of a warm bath made my spirits rise considerably. I took my soap, shampoo, and a clean tunic, and headed downstairs to find the innkeeper. I wasn't going to spend one more night in the bedroom he'd given us unless it was completely washed, aired out, and new sheets were put on the beds.

Finding the man wasn't difficult; I just followed the sound of his bellowing. After I'd straightened things out with him, I tucked my bath things under my arm and headed towards the baths. I was sure I'd find Alexander there, and I was right. The Greeks, as I've said before, loved cleanliness.

Plexis and Alexander were in deep discussion. I smiled as I approached and they both looked up at me.

'Well, finally awake?' Plexis said. 'Not too tired?'

'Very tired,' I admitted, sitting next to them. 'I hardly slept, the bed was dreadful. Didn't the fleas bother you? And the sheets weren't clean. I gave orders to the ...' My voice trailed off. The two men weren't listening. Plexis had a frown on his face and was staring over my shoulder while Alexander examined something on the inside of his wrist.

'What is it?' I asked, looking from one to the other.

Alexander said, 'Nearchus wants to leave us and go to Africa.'

'We're heading towards Carthage,' I said.

'No, he wants to leave the inner sea and travel down the coast from the exterior ocean, the one you call the Atlantic.'

'What, by himself?'

'No, he's gone to the harbour to find a boat. Last night he heard someone talking about exploring the coast and it got him thinking.' Alexander spoke sadly. I could understand why.

The thought of losing Nearchus was painful. He'd always been around, tall, silent, and serious. I glanced over at Plexis. His face was tight. They were very close friends. Then I turned to Alexander. I knew what Nearchus felt for him, but Alexander's feelings had always been more ambiguous.

'What are you thinking?' he asked me.

'I was thinking about how much I was going to miss him,' I said, and I was surprised by the catch in my voice.

'We'll all miss him.' Alexander pulled me down onto his lap. 'He'll meet us in Alexandria in one year,' he said.

'Is that enough time to explore the coast, do you think?' asked Plexis, frowning at me.

'It should be,' I said cautiously. 'But it's a very dangerous place, full of warring tribes and wild animals.'

'He wants to talk to you about it,' said Alexander. 'He wants you to help him plan his voyage.'

My shoulders sagged. 'I never went to Africa. It's one of the forbidden places.'

'But you know the contours of the land, the distances, the dangers, and you can warn him what things to look out for. Please, Ashley, he needs you.'

'I'll do my best, I promise.' I sat up and took Alexander's face in my hand. I tilted it a bit, so that the sun shone on it. I smiled. 'Don't worry, I think if anyone can sail around Africa at this time it's Nearchus. Does he have a boat?'

'He will find one, I'm sure, by the time the week's up. After he leaves, we must make haste to Carthage. I want to get there before the ceremonies.' Alexander's gaze never wavered from mine.

I leaned over and kissed him, then straightened up and looked towards the bathhouse. 'It's time for the women to bathe – shall I see you back at the inn for lunch?'

'If we're not at the inn, go to the port; we'll be with the dragon boat,' said Plexis, standing up and stretching. His eyes were shadowed, his face pensive. I thought he was still thinking about Nearchus, and I was right.

In the bath, it hit me. Plexis was caught in a dilemma. On one hand he longed to go with Nearchus and sail around the coast of Africa, seeing for himself the incredible sights I'd told them about. On the other hand he wanted to stay with Alexander and me, especially since I was carrying his child and would give birth in less than five months. When I finished bathing and returned to the inn, Plexis was alone in our room, standing near the window. I had opened the door quietly but he heard me. A smile tugged at his lips.

'I wanted to speak to you,' he said softly. He took my toilet case from my hand, set it on the commode, and then motioned me to sit on the bed. He sat on the floor at my feet, his arms on my knees, his hands folded over my thighs. 'I want to go with Nearchus, but I cannot.'

'You can if you really want to, you know that. I would never begrudge you the voyage,' I said, stroking his glossy curls.

'I know that, but I cannot go. I could never leave you, especially in your condition.'

'Are you sorry I'm pregnant?' I asked him. A stab of worry made me turn my face away. I didn't want him to see my distress.

'No, you can't believe that. I'm happy, and Iskander is happy. No, it's not for that reason that I won't go. But I do admit to wanting to. It's a strange feeling I have, as if Nearchus ...' He broke off. 'You know how I get these funny feelings sometimes. And often they turn out to be absolutely nothing.'

'But sometimes they come true. Is that why you're worried? Do you think Nearchus will be in danger?'

'I'd be a fool not to think that. Why, just going to Carthage will be dangerous. That must be the explanation. The danger is real and I feel it keenly, that's all.'

'Why did you want to talk to me?'

'You know I never ask you about the future. But I wanted to know if you remembered anything from your history books about Nearchus. Does he die in Africa? Can you tell me that?' His voice was halting.

I looked at him. His tone was strange, but I put it down to his worry about Nearchus. 'I'm sorry, I don't know anything about that. I can't recall anything else besides the fact that he was Iskander's admiral, and that he wrote a book about the trip he took from the mouth of the Indus to Babylon.'

'He's already published that, I know, because he left the manuscript in Alexandria and Ptolemy was going to take care of it. It will be one of the books in the modern section of the new library there.'

'The modern section?' My mouth twitched.

Plexis nodded, an answering smile on his lips. I looked down at him, and the feeling that had been growing in my belly made me close my eyes again, but this time it wasn't pain, unless sharp desire can be called pain.

Plexis knew what I was feeling. His hands slid over my thighs and grasped my hips, and he pulled himself up and onto me. His mouth sought mine, his hands roamed over my body, caressing me. His breath grew harsher and deepened. 'Two months on a crowded boat is too long,' he

43

murmured. 'I missed making love to you, I missed the taste of you, the feel of you, and the ... oh, by Eros, I, I can't talk any more.'

'Then don't.' I arched my back and welcomed him in, my own breath catching in my throat and leaving it with a cry. 'Harder,' I gasped, then said nothing as the feelings crested over me and I was swept away by the movement of his hips.

There was a moment of silence, when we both stopped breathing and moving, savouring the sensations that joined us as one. Then the wave broke and we shuddered together. It made him cry out, as if he were in pain, but I knew better, he always fought against losing himself, and when it happened it shook him to his very bones. Afterwards we held each other. The tremors in my body answered his. His hair was damp with sweat and his breathing came in deep shudders.

'Shh, there now. Hold me. Hold me tightly, Plexis. Oh, how I love you. Look at your arm, it's shaking.'

'How could I leave you?' he asked, and his voice was rough with emotion.

'And yet, I would never hold you back. If you want to go, you must.'

'No, I want to stay. We will travel to Africa together. Life is long; we have years and years before us. We shall wait for Nearchus to come home, and then he'll take us to the places he loved best.' He was silent for a moment, resting next to me, his hand on my belly, his head pressed to mine. 'What was that?' he whispered, raising his head and looking down at his hand.

'Did you feel it?'

'The baby moved, was that what I just felt? It was like, I don't know, as if you had a butterfly in your stomach, just there. Oh! It moved again,' he laughed weakly and bent his head down to kiss the soft swelling of my belly. 'Hello,' he whispered. 'Can you hear me? It's your father. I'm right here.' He lay his cheek against my stomach and smiled when he felt the tiny movement stir against his skin. Tears fell from his closed eyes. I stroked his head and said nothing.

We stayed in Iberia for three days, then Nearchus found a swift boat and sailed away from us, leaving one morning with the wind coming from the east. The sun had just cleared the horizon, and its light was shell pink and tender on the boat's white sails. Nearchus stood on the deck, one hand on the mast, the other raised in a salute. He didn't say anything, but his face glittered, as did ours, with tears.

We waved. We called farewell and wept bitterly as his ship left the harbour and dwindled in the distance. For an hour we stood watching, then when his sail was nothing but a small bright triangle on the horizon, we turned and made our way back to our boat. We were leaving too, but in the opposite direction, and it was the west wind that would take us across the Mediterranean towards Carthage.

The boat was soon loaded and our baggage stowed away. The inn had been expensive but we'd traded well, and Alexander was able to pay and still have money left over.

We were silent as we stepped on board, and silent as we raised the sails and cast off. In the purple evening, the air was cool. The villages along the coast started to light their lamps and soon they were all we could see.

Before the lights of the town were lost to us in the evening mist, Vix sacrificed a young goat, first scattering barley over its head, then cutting its throat. Half the goat was burned in honour of the gods on Olympus and half was thrown into the sea to appease Poseidon. Vix then filled a silver chalice with wine and poured it into the water while singing a chant invoking the clemency of the gods for our journey. Another goat was sacrificed, this time to slake our appetites, and Erati grilled morsels of meat and basted them with flame-coloured wine. In the purple dusk, we ate our dinner. Then we sat in a circle of lamplight and talked softly, our voices hardly rising above the whisper of wind in the sails.

'He had been wanting to go for so long,' said Alexander. 'Even before we left for Gaul he started planning. But he came with us.'

'And now he's gone.' Plexis spoke with a sigh. The lamplight made shadows on our faces. 'I hope your map will help him,' he said to me.

I didn't answer. My throat was too tight. I remembered the last night we'd spent in the inn, sitting around a low table, examining the map I'd drawn from memory, speaking about all the possible dangers. I was afraid that I'd forgotten something vital, something that he would need to know, and it worried me.

'Your help was immense,' said Alexander, taking my face in his hands and looking into my eyes. 'Just the map would have been enough. But you also told him about the natives and the animals. He will return, have no fear. He will sail down the coast to the Equator then come back home. He promised, and besides, the crew with him will want to go no further.'

'He'll want to go on,' I whispered, pressing closer to him. 'He'll ask to go on alone, he'll go on foot if he has to. I know him; he won't even care if he dies there. His heart is broken, it broke the day Plexis came to Orce.'

Alexander shook his head. 'No, you don't know Nearchus.' He pulled me to his chest and held me.

'I'm sorry,' I said. 'I shouldn't have said anything. Maybe it's all my fault.'

'It matters not,' he said firmly. 'You're wrong, Plexis never broke his heart, and neither did you.'

'Then you did,' I said sadly. 'I saw it in his face, before he left. He was so sorrowful.'

'That's why he will come back,' said Alexander. 'He'll come back because he will miss me.'

We slept on deck, in the shelter of the cabin, as we often did when the weather was fair. Beneath us was a pallet of hay covered with smooth linen, above us were the twinkling stars, and all around was the vast sea, slapping gently against the hull, as the boat rose and fell with the waves.

Chapter Three

One week later, we sailed into the harbour in Carthage. I got my first glimpse of the fabled city at noon. The sun flashed on the wonderful mosaics and glittered off the billions of scintillating tiles covering the pillars and houses. The mosaics and tiles were amazing, with deep hues of turquoise, blues and greens, pepper-hot reds, oranges, and all the golds and yellows of the sun. The effect was glorious.

The harbour was deep and very grand, as Carthage was a seaport. At her back was the endless desert, in front, her arms curled around the water like a mother holding a child. Some caravans did come from the arid wasteland, bringing gold and strange spices and skins to trade, but most everyone came to Carthage by the sea.

Boats of all shapes and sizes bobbed in the harbour. In front of the Imperial Palace, protected by a jetty that cut the harbour in two, was the Imperial Fleet of triremes, low, sleek warships, all with sharp prows, triple levels of rowers, beautifully weighted keels, able to change direction forwards or backwards, instantly. They were guarded by armed soldiers and ready to leave at a moment's notice, day or night.

The Imperial Palace took up a good part of the peninsula reaching out on the left side of the bay as you looked at Carthage, your back to the sea. On the right were the customs buildings, the trading docks, the unloading and loading piers, and the fish markets.

In the harbour, was a small island girdled by a sandy beach. A temple was built upon it. A humped stone bridge led to the island from the centre of the waterfront. There were no docks on the island. Just a wide, golden beach surrounded by jumbled boulders. An arched stone gate with an iron door stood on the island side of the bridge. The door was closed. The temple was deserted. We couldn't even sail close to the island. Sharp rocks sticking out of the water guarded it.

The wind was brisk, so we manoeuvred the boat carefully. A dragon boat attracted attention, and a customs boat had come out to intercept us before we even entered the harbour. Once he saw we were traders, he escorted us to our mooring.

Phaleria immediately set about unloading the goods she wanted to sell while Alexander, Axiom, Plexis, Yovanix, Paul, and I set out to explore the city.

The city rose steeply above the bay, with many streets turning into wide staircases. The houses were large, airy, and terraced. Date palms and fruit trees grew in parks and lined the streets. Fountains were everywhere, sparkling and splashing in every garden and square.

Yovanix walked surely, one hand resting lightly on Paul's shoulder, the other holding the new leash Plexis had woven for Perilous. The dog was growing fast, and his training was coming along well. Docile now, and obedient, he trotted just ahead of Yovanix, slowing whenever an obstacle presented itself. An obstacle could be a large pothole, a curb, stairs, or whatever else risked making Yovanix lose his balance and fall.

Plexis walked next to the dog and corrected him when he did something wrong, and Paul was there to steady Yovanix, in case the puppy forgot himself and leapt after a cat. But the puppy was behaving beautifully, and Paul could concentrate instead on describing what we were seeing as we walked from the docks into the city.

'We're following a wide avenue that leads slightly uphill and curves around to the left, hugging the shore. On our right are houses and shops, and on our left is a wall, about shoulder level, beyond which is the sea.'

'I can hear the waves breaking against the seawall,' said Yovanix, 'and we've just passed a fishmonger. I could smell his weekly special.' He wrinkled his nose. 'I don't think I'd want to eat it.'

Paul grinned. 'Now we're in front of the harbour. Ahead of us are the Imperial Palace gates, about a hundred metres away, I'd say. To our right is a huge arch, and through it is a bridge leading to the temple on the island.'

'I can feel the wind coming through the arch,' said Yovanix, turning his banded eyes towards it. The breeze blew his light brown hair off his high forehead, showing the white skin. He smiled, tilting his head. 'I can hear the difference between the waves hitting the rocks and the waves washing up on the sandy beach.'

'There is no one on the island,' I said, 'Why?'

'Only the priests go when they perform their ceremonies,' said Axiom. He looked at the sky. 'I believe it's going to rain.'

'It won't rain for a while yet,' said Alexander, glancing at the heavy clouds on the horizon.

'To our right is a wide street. It's at right angles to the waterfront and it cuts the city in half. It seems to be the main street, with many other smaller ones leading off from it.' Paul said to Yovanix.

'We can take the main street and see if we can find lodgings.' Alexander took my arm. 'Shall we?'

'We shall,' I said.

Paul continued his guided tour for Yovanix. 'The houses are made of stone and wood, with mosaics covering every available space. The streets are paved with flat flagstones – watch your step there; that stone is broken. The houses here are not very grand. Up on the top of the hill are bigger residences, and I can see two or three behind formidable walls. I can only catch a glimpse of their rooftops, but they look to be quite huge. They must be the palaces and the wealthy quarters.'

Yovanix turned his head, listening to Paul and trying to sense where he was going. The street sloped gently upwards. Sometimes there would be a shallow step in the road. The puppy was learning to stop at these to give Yovanix time to 'see' it with his foot.

'There's a public garden on our left, and up ahead the street widens and circles a fountain, probably a sacred spring. There is a small temple built over it, and bouquets of flowers have been deposited all around it.'

'I smell the flowers,' said Yovanix. He spoke evenly, with no sign of the strain he must be feeling. His hand on Paul's shoulder was firm but gentle. 'And on our left there is a bakery. The bread has just come out of the oven.'

'That's right! Can we buy some, Father? I'm starving.' Paul looked at Alexander pleadingly and Alexander flipped his wrist and took a coin out of his purse.

'Get some sweet buns for all of us,' he said. 'You're not the only starving voyager here.'

We sat on a tiled bench in the public garden and ate our buns. They were warm, fragrant with honey, and covered with toasted sesame seeds. We ate the buns, licked our fingers, and did some people-watching.

'There goes a woman riding a donkey. She's wearing a red robe and a yellow shawl fringed with glass beads; that's making the clicking noise you hear. She looks like she's in a hurry – she probably has an appointment at the beauty parlour and she's late.' Paul leaned forwards and said, 'I see three men carrying a long, rolled-up rug. It looks heavy. I bet it's for one of the houses on the hill. The men are wearing identical blue loincloths. They must be slaves, working in the same household. Now I see a young girl with long black hair reaching down to her knees. She has a gold circlet on her head. She is escorted by two eunuchs. They are wearing long robes, and, oh! One just billowed in the breeze and I saw a huge, curved sword at his waist.'

'That's called a scimitar, and it's quite deadly, I assure you.' said Plexis.

Paul whistled. 'It *looks* deadly! There are at least fifty women shopping in this street. They are carrying most of their goods in baskets made of woven grass. The baskets have large handles that loop over their shoulders.'

'Shall we go to find some place to shelter?' asked Alexander. 'I think it's going to rain.'

A fat raindrop fell with a loud plop, landing in the soft dust at our feet. Axiom and I looked up at the clouds. 'I thought you said it wouldn't rain until later,' I said to Alexander.

Axiom grinned. 'I think I see an inn over there, see? Where the third street on the left connects to the main street.'

We hurried to the shelter of the inn, arriving just as the heavens opened and a deluge suddenly obscured the harbour from our view. The innkeeper rented us two small but clean rooms overlooking the bay. Our room had an oil lamp made of pale blue glass hanging from the ceiling. The breeze made it swing. The shadows around us reared and subsided as the lamp moved back and forth. Outside, the night was full of noise. The city never slept. Restaurants were crowded with people, and the streets were busy. In the cool of the evening, the city started to bustle.

We ate early and retired to our rooms. The fatigue of the journey made our movements torpid. I lay on my back on the bed and watched the lamp, melancholy washing through me.

'Are you thinking of the tent?' asked Alexander, stretching out by my side.

'I suppose so. We're almost home, aren't we? Just two more stops, and then home at last.'

He sighed deeply. 'It seems as if we've been travelling for ten years, instead of just one. The memories of Orce are already confused with those of Britain and Gaul. Sometimes I dream of the old woman who leaned over the pit where I was kept prisoner. I see a wizened crone, and then her face changes and she becomes Olympias. And sometimes I forget how you lost your hand. I look at your arm, and I get confused.' He was silent, thinking.

'I hardly remember that either,' I said. It was true, the memory was diffused by shock. I could only recall the smell of my flesh being cauterized, and Demos's voice crooning in my ear. The rest was a blur. Mostly I tried not to think about the accident that cost me my left hand. It *had* been an accident, after all. My son hadn't meant to hurt me. It was my fault; I'd tried to grab a razor-sharp sword.

The lamp swung back and forth in front of my vision, its flame flickering and dimming. The room darkened. Outside, a rush of wind clattered the shutters, rustled the palm fronds, and drowned out the murmur of voices coming from downstairs. My heart beat irregularly. Sometimes it did that when I was too tired or stressed. Other times my nose bled. Not tonight, though. No sharp tickle warned me of a nosebleed, so I closed my eyes and breathed slowly.

Beside me, Alexander stirred. 'Babylon seems so far away,' he said softly. 'That's another thing I keep forgetting – my own death there. It was such a lovely city, though tinged with sorrow. I wonder why, with all the beauty, I can only remember the tears?'

'"*How many miles to Babylon? Three score miles and ten. Can I get there by candlelight? Yes, and back again*",' I quoted in a murmur. I didn't open my eyes. Visions of the city overwhelmed me. I saw the gate of Ishtar, its blue enamelled tiles glowing in the sun. The great ziggurat that rose above the city like a fantastic, pink spaceship. The temples and courtyards, the central marketplace with its striped awnings, fountains, and white camels. An amber river flowed through the city, cutting the palace in two, irrigating the hanging gardens with its precious water. I envisioned the palace with its echoing brick hallways and huge, arched passages. The biggest rooms had been built below the ground in the cool entrails of the earth. My room had overlooked a small courtyard where an emerald pool sparkled in the middle of towering palm trees. Lined with deep green tiles, the pool was always cool and inviting. Each evening, I'd swum in it, feeling the water like silk caressing me. Or maybe it was Alexander's hand.

'You're crying,' he said, bending over to kiss my tears away. 'Why? What did that poem mean?'

'I don't know,' I said. 'It was already older than dust when I learned it.'

'Why aren't you sleeping?'

'I'm having a hard time falling asleep,' I admitted. 'Perhaps that's why I'm crying. I'm just exhausted, and I can't sleep.'

'Time, what a strange thing,' he said meditatively. 'It flows by like water, never stopping, never looking back. Yet you defied it, breasted the current, and returned upstream to a time not your own. The people of your day have no idea what they're really doing, do they? I used to think of them as time gods. Now I only pity them.'

I opened my eyes. He was leaning over me, his face hidden in darkness. Only his eyes glittered.

'Why?' I asked.

'Because I have you, they do not. Don't be sad, Ashley of the Sacred Sandals. You are here, and wherever or whenever that is, it's enough to have you with me.'

I smiled then. Sleep was nudging me, but so was something else. Something near my hip. My throat tightened suddenly. My flesh contracted with a shiver of delight, and Alexander laughed softly.

'It's enough for me too,' I said, 'and it always has been.' I sighed. 'Mmm, that feels good.'

'I think I know of a good way to help you sleep,' he said. The lamplight was blotted out as he moved on top of me, and I closed my eyes and let his body sing me to sleep.

Chapter Four

In the morning, quiet calm had replaced my melancholy. I sat before the mirror and let one of the inn's slaves dress my hair. My reflection stared back at me. My eyes were still pale blue and my hair a sweep of silver. The bones in my face had changed subtly though. The past year had added depth to the hollows beneath my cheeks and slanted my eyes even more. They had lost their icy frost, but they were far from warm. The Viking blood was even more apparent now, my mouth was still wide, but the lips were less generous than before. I was thirty-two. In this time I was considered middle-aged, and although I looked younger than most people my age, I didn't look like the youthful girl Alexander had mistaken for Hades' bride. Four pregnancies had changed my body, and sorrow had marked my face.

I watched in silence as the slave woman braided my tresses and wove tiny, blue glass beads into them. I wasn't a vain person. I hadn't really looked at a mirror in nearly a year. Perhaps that was why I was taking such careful stock of myself now. The cream I put on my face every day kept my skin soft. The fact that I didn't have to do hard work helped keep me strong. I'd worn hats to shade my face, and I'd never gone sunbathing, another plus for my skin. I'd always had enough to eat, and even if I was thin compared to future standards, it was a healthy slim. My teeth were still good, I was fanatically careful about cleaning them, and not eating sweets helped immensely.

I glanced at the woman busy braiding my hair. She was from Carthage and I didn't speak any Phoenician, so I couldn't converse with her. I'd asked her name. After a pause, she'd replied Sorra. Her voice had been shy. She took my hand and gave me a manicure; I couldn't do it myself any more, having just one hand. Then she gave me a pedicure and helped me lace up my sandals. She was a perfect lady's maid, helping me pick out a robe and draping it expertly over my shoulders. She was shorter than I and had to reach up to fasten the fibula. When she was done, she stepped back and looked me over. Then she nodded, satisfied, and gave me a wide smile.

I went to the terrace. The sun was fully risen and the harbour was crowded with boats. It was early and the market stands had unfolded their awnings and were doing a brisk business. Below me were a fishmonger, a glassmaker, a leather worker, and a man selling vegetables. Another man was selling parrots, and they added their loud screeching to the din.

The morning was just starting. I draped my cloak over my shoulders and went downstairs. Alexander, Plexis, and everyone else had gone to the boat at daybreak to help Phaleria. They would work and trade until noon, and then we'd meet here, at the inn, for lunch. I was free to do as I liked, and I wanted to stroll around. It had been forever, it seemed, since I was on my own in a lovely city with nothing to do but explore and enjoy the scenery. An exhilarating sense of freedom swept over me as I stepped into the thronging streets. I smiled then, from pure joy, and headed up the hill. I wanted to see the view from above. I also wanted a glimpse of the Imperial Palace. I thought I'd be able to see it better from the hilltop.

The climb was steep and my legs hurt by the time I reached the summit. At the very top, a temple had been built overlooking the city. I didn't think women were allowed inside, so I walked around the exterior, peeking over the tall wall when I could and admiring the gardens. I saw priests but no worshippers. The priests wore dark blue pagnes, Greek-style, and shaved their heads. There were three of them, kneeling in front of a statue of a bull, praying loudly in a strange tongue. The sun beat on their heads but they didn't move. After a while I grew tired of watching them, and I walked further along the stone causeway, stopping now and then to gaze at the lapis blue sea with white and yellow sails dotting it.

The city was busy that day. From what we gathered, it was preparing to fête Carthage's victory over Tartessos, and also the new sovereignty. Today the island in the middle of the harbour was being decked with flowers. Hundreds of blossoms were being tied onto the columns and pillars with bright red ribbons. It looked as if the sparkling white pillars were dripping scarlet ribbons of blood. I shuddered with a chill in the hot sun. The image of a white bull came to me, and I remembered Phaleria's tale of the sacrifice she had seen in this city when she was a child. I turned and went back along the cobblestone path, intending to return to the city and get something to drink. My throat was dry.

As I passed the wall again I glanced over it, expecting to see the priests bowed in prayer. But what I saw was a youth lying on top of the statue.

At first, I didn't realize what I was seeing. The boy was struggling gamely, trying to escape, but he was firmly tied to the stone bull. In a way, he looked as if he were trying to fornicate with it and, if it weren't for the grimly determined look on his face, I might have giggled. The look on his face, and the implication of his plight, stopped me from laughing. The sacrificial victims were presented to the god on the back of a bull. This boy was about twelve years old. He was wiry and strong, but not strong enough to break free. I saw that in an instant. That didn't stop him from trying. Sweat beaded his brow, and tendons stood out in his throat and arms. Finally, with a sob, he stopped and just lay there, panting mightily. His face was turned towards me, and our eyes met. He froze. In his gaze was utter despair.

I realized that I was standing with my hand pressed to the top of the wall, which was roughly chin level. I'd been holding my breath so long my chest hurt. A green flash caught my eye and I bent down and picked up a piece of tile, broken off the wall. The tile was made of baked glass, and the shard I held was long and sharp as a knife.

I don't think I understood for an instant what I was doing. If I had thought about it, I would have continued down the hill and later cried in Alexander's arms. But I didn't think. I shucked off my robe and vaulted over the wall, holding the glass sliver in my teeth, my good hand clutching the hot stone.

I cleared the wall and sprang at the boy. His mouth gaped and his eyes bulged, but he didn't cry out. Behind him, in the deep shade of a cypress tree, I saw a priest kneeling and heard him chanting. He didn't hear me, because he was facing the other way. All I saw of him was his back, swaying slowly back and forth in rhythm with the prayer.

Axiom would be furious, I remember thinking, as I neatly cut through the boy's ropes and set him free. He was always telling me not to get involved or protest at other people's religions. However, this was murder, I told myself, not religion. The boy and I breached the wall in silence under a white-hot sky. On the other side, I put my robe back on and threw the glass shard as far into the underbrush as possible. It sparkled like an emerald in the light, then disappeared.

The boy and I stared at each other. He stood still, rubbing the red welts on his arms. Then the priest stopped chanting, turned, and uttered a high shriek.

My first instinct was to run, but there was only one narrow path along here, and there was nowhere to hide. Instead, I lifted my robe and pushed the boy beneath it. He clung to my legs, his whole body vibrating with fear.

A second later a man with a donkey topped the rise, and two slave women holding earthenware jars on their heads, followed. Inside the temple, there was pandemonium, and those passing by stopped, of course, and peered over the wall to see what the matter was. I could only do the same.

So there we were, a man with a donkey, two slave women, and a blonde woman in red robes, looking over the wall. The priests rushed by us, asking breathlessly if anyone had seen a boy, about so high, running away.

The man with the donkey raised his eyebrows and said 'no', emphatically. The slave women shook their heads, and so did I, looking as puzzled as possible.

The priests ran on, and the man with the donkey turned to me and said something in Phoenician which I didn't understand, so I just shrugged and shook my head. He seemed satisfied and shook his head as well. He must have said something like, 'What a terrible event!' The two slave women turned and carried their jars towards their home, and the man with the donkey continued along his path. I leaned against the wall and shook just as hard as the boy huddled between my legs.

When the coast was clear, I tore my cloak in two and put one half on the boy's head like a turban and one around his waist as a loin cloth. He became my slave boy, dressed in the colours of his master, carrying a large jar I hastily purchased from the first merchant we met.

The priests passed us several times on our way down the hill. They glanced at me, but then again, everyone did. I was tall and blonde and tended to stand out. However, they didn't look twice at the slave boy carrying my goods. And the boy was careful to hide his face each time they passed. The priests would soon have the entire city stirred up, so I headed directly to the docks, towards the boat. It was the only thing I could think of doing at the moment. To go back to the inn would be folly; the innkeeper would be suspicious of a new slave. There was no one I knew living in Carthage at that time, the only person I'd ever met who'd even been to Carthage was Phaleria, perhaps she'd know what to do.

'What to do?' she cried, her face drained of all colour. 'Are you mad? Have you lost your senses? This boy is the sacrifice for tomorrow's victory celebration! Of course we can't keep him! Soon the whole harbour will be sealed off, and the soldiers will search each house and boat looking for him. We can't keep him here, we'll all be executed!'

'We can't turn him in,' I said desperately, 'they'll kill him!'

'He was chosen by the Snake God,' hissed Phaleria, pacing back and forth in the small space of the cabin, her eyes frightened.

'The who?'

'The Snake God. The priests select several youths especially for the sacrifice. The boys stand together on woven grass mats, and the sacred cobra slithers out of the basket. The one the Snake God touches is chosen.' She'd barely finished speaking when a trumpet blew from the palace. Its sound was taken up by others until the whole city was full of sound.

'I'm sorry. I wasn't thinking, but Phaleria, we can't give him back, they'll kill him!'

'I know,' she spoke as if she were speaking with a slightly simple child. 'I know that. I was here before. I saw what happens. The boy rides a white bull to the temple on the island. Scarlet and white ribbons are tied to the bull's horns and the boy's hair. The ribbons flutter in the breeze.

Then the boy is helped off the bull. A priest cuts off a lock of his hair and throws it into the sacred fire. The boy is tied to the wooden post and then ...' Her voice trailed away.

'And then he's burned alive,' I finished for her, my own voice gentle.

'He was so beautiful,' said Phaleria, her hand coming to her mouth. 'I was only fifteen and the boy was not much older. I saw him and fell in love with him instantly. I was infatuated, the way a fifteen-year-old girl can become infatuated with a boy after just one glance. He turned his head and our eyes met. His dark eyes were filled with fear and hopelessness. When he saw me his face changed. My feelings must have shone from my face like a beacon, and it gave him hope. It was the worst thing I could have done. Suddenly he began to struggle to escape. His eyes never left mine, even when the priests surrounded him and carried him, kicking and yelling hoarsely, to the pyre. When they cut off a lock of his hair, they cut his temple, and I can remember the red blood streaming down his face. He kept screaming, over and over, words I couldn't understand. And then they burned him.'

Phaleria looked at her fists and unclenched them. Bright red crescents marked where her nails had dug into her palms. She studied the boy. He was staring at her with an intensity that was painful. He didn't speak our language, but he understood what was happening. His fate was being decided again.

'All right,' she said. 'All right. We'll try to hide him. By the gods, Ashley, you're putting us in danger. If he's caught we'll all burn; you, me, Iskander, Paul, Demos, Plexis,

Axiom, and Yovanix.' Each name received the weight of her fear behind it, and I saw them already dead, already executed for my action. However, my eyes kept straying to the thin shadow in the corner, the quiet boy with the burning eyes, and I smiled.

'You weren't with us in India,' I said.

'No, what do you have in mind?'

'I need one of our glass fishing buoys, lead weights, and strong rope. If we can get these, the soldiers can tear the boat apart and they will never find him.'

The rest was easy; Alexander and Demos rigged a diving bell from a buoy, and Axiom fixed the weights to it using the rope and intricate knots. No one protested, once the plan was set out. Everyone was ready to sacrifice his life.

Plexis, Axiom, and Alexander spoke Phoenician fluently. The boy heard what he had to do. He nodded, his eyes shining. The only expression in them was relief. When the Imperial Soldiers and priests came to our boat, we were ready.

They were thorough. They searched methodically, emptying the boat and tapping the planks, looking for a secret hiding place. They used long, thin knives, poking them systematically into sacks of grain and bales of wool. They put all boats under temporary arrest, blocked the harbour, and closed the inns. Private homes were searched with the same zeal, and the people who were near the temple when the boy disappeared were taken to the Imperial Palace for questioning. The boy wasn't found, for who would think of looking for him underwater?

Chapter Five

Next morning I dressed carefully in order to go to the Imperial Palace to answer the summons of the royal guard. I was a suspect in the case of the missing sacrificial victim.

I said that jokingly to Axiom and he shook his head sorrowfully. No one was smiling that morning except the boy we'd saved. He peered out of the hiding place we'd made for him and his grin was as wide as the ocean. Phaleria caught him with his head poking out and hissed at him, making him disappear back into his corner behind a false wall.

I watched in silence as Alexander put on my false hand, lacing it up and giving it a little shake. The fun was missing from his eyes as well. He looked tense, and when a slave dropped an amphora of wine onto the stone jetty, he jumped.

'What is it?' I asked.

He shook his head. 'Never have I heard of a sacrificial victim being saved. What will the gods think?'

'You know what I think?' I said darkly, meaning to tell him just exactly what I thought, but he pressed his finger against my lips.

'No. No, Ashley. This is one of the times that the gulf separating us is too great to be crossed. We are all frightened of the gods' choler. Only you are free of them.'

'What about Plexis? He doesn't seem frightened.'

'You know Plexis. He should have been an actor.'

Plexis went with me as my lawyer, and to translate. He put on his finest tunic and wore a gold circlet in his dark hair. He looked like a prince, and the people at the palace were suitably deferential.

The man with the donkey and the two slave women were there, as well as at least twenty other people. One I recognized as the merchant who'd sold me the jar of oil.

Luckily, he didn't make the connection between the escaped sacrificial victim and my slave boy. To complete the masquerade, we dressed Paul as a slave. He wore a red loincloth and a red turban hid his golden hair. He walked behind us, fanning me with a graceful fan made of white egret feathers.

The palace was huge. Slaves led us to a large, luxurious room. One wall was covered with small cubbyholes where the tasselled ends of scrolls were visible. There must have been five hundred scrolls there – an incredible fortune. A statue graced another corner. It was Greek, made of white marble painted realistically. It made me pause. I wasn't used to seeing statues painted that way, although Plexis assured me that it was how they did it in Athens. The eyes were set with dark blue stone, the lips were painted red, and the robes blue.

Tapestries covered the floor. On the walls, mosaics depicting life in Carthage, with brilliantly coloured birds and flowers made of semi-precious stones and glass, glittered in the sunlight that flooded the room from large windows. There was so much to look at that I was still gaping when the heavy, ornately carved door swung open and a thin man stepped in, his face creased with worry. He carried a scroll in one hand and a gold sceptre in the other. For a minute I thought he might be the king, but no, he bowed to us, something a king never does, and motioned for me to take a seat.

I sat on a large cushion placed in the middle of the floor and nodded towards my 'slave' boy to remain behind me. Plexis stood on my right, on his face a look of polite interest.

The man introduced himself, Scipio Atticas, counsellor for the prince Hamilcar, who was the commander of the army. His face didn't lose its painful tightness during the entire interview. He spoke to me, waiting for Plexis to translate. He watched me closely as I spoke and then listened gravely as Plexis gave him my answer.

'Where were you yesterday at the time of the escape?' was his first question.

'I was taking a walk along the small path which leads along the crest of the hill.'

'Did you see a young boy leap over the wall at any point?'

'No, I saw only a few people; a man with a donkey, two women with clay jars on their heads, and some other persons. I didn't really take any notice.'

'And where was your slave all this time? The man with the donkey said he wasn't with you when the alert was given. The merchant further down the road said he was with you when you bought the oil.'

'The boy was hot. I let him rest in the shade. I gave him instructions not to make a pest of himself. He must have fallen asleep. I found him exactly where I'd left him. He came with me to buy some oil and he carried it back to the boat.'

The counsellor looked at his scroll and nodded. 'Everything you said has been corroborated by different witnesses, and your boat was found to be hiding no boy. You are therefore free to go.'

'Thank you,' I said, rising from my cushion.

'I hope you will attend the ceremony. For the trouble we have caused you, we are extending an invitation to the sacred island.'

I watched Plexis as he translated this, and he looked as startled as I felt. However, he made a subtle gesture with his hand, meaning I should agree.

'It's a great honour,' I said. Almost as an afterthought, I asked, 'What will happen now? Is there another victim?'

Plexis coughed delicately, and nearly didn't translate. The man paused for a long time before answering. 'The boy who escaped will be replaced by my only son if we don't find him. That is why I have been appointed to investigate. You see, they know I will do everything in my power to discover where he's gone. My own boy's life is at stake.'

Plexis translated as he spoke, so there was no time for him to soften the blow of the words. We discovered the truth at the same time, and stared, horrified, at the man. He looked at us and a wry smile flickered over his face. 'I love my son. He is all I have left since his mother died. I must admit, I was hoping that your slave would turn out to be the escaped boy, but I saw right away it wasn't.' He bowed, indicating the interview was over.

We walked back to the boat through crowded streets, the orange sun setting at our backs, casting long shadows before us. I couldn't feel my feet hitting the ground. I was suffocating with the horror of what I'd done. 'Now what?' I asked, when I found my voice.

'What do you mean, "now what"? We make our excuses not to go to the ceremony, and we sail away, that's what,' said Plexis forcibly.

'No.' I put my hand to my face and wiped away the blood that had started to trickle from my nose. 'Give me a handkerchief, will you? No, we can't go. That man is going to lose his son by my fault. I won't stand by and let that happen.'

We were silent for the rest of the walk. As Plexis had so pointedly once said, 'The streets have ears.'

Once back in the boat, I sought Alexander. If anyone could save a prisoner from the palace it had to be him. He'd planned more battles than anyone else I'd ever known. He was always talking strategies, a tone of regret in his voice, as he looked at a fortress or unbreachable wall. I told him what had happened, my voice shaking with sorrow. He listened as he always did, giving me his full attention. When I finished speaking, he tilted his head to the side,

70

thinking. A dreamy look had come into his eyes, and he was almost smiling.

'We may all get killed,' he said reflectively, 'but I think it can be done.' He said no more, but went to find Demos. I heard him mutter softly to himself, 'Damn Nearchus, never around when I really need him ...' Then he was gone. I sank onto a bench. I couldn't get the man's face out of my head. His eyes had been so bleak. His only son, he'd said. I shuddered.

In the morning, an official came to the inn and delivered an invitation to the ceremony. He was accompanied by two drummers, and the innkeeper stared at Alexander and me with awe. Not many people had been invited to the sacred island, the innkeeper told us after the official had gone. We pretended to be suitably impressed.

That evening, the trumpets of the city blew brassy swan cries through the still air, announcing the start of the ceremonies. Criers ran through the streets shouting the news. *The Snake God had chosen a new sacrificial victim!* People, dressed in their finest clothes, gathered in family groups. The streets were packed with revellers and musicians, jugglers and acrobats. We were submerged in the crowd. I held onto Alexander's arm with a hand that was as cold as ice despite the thick heat of the evening air. Everyone was pouring down towards the harbour, eager to get places along the sea wall to better see the sacrifice.

Alexander and I were the only ones from our boat going to the ceremony. Everyone else had a role to play. Paul was obliged to be a slave to the very end, so, dressed in his slave garb, he stayed on board the ship. He acted glum, as if all he'd wanted to do was watch the ceremony, and here he was stuck on a boat. The crew, Kell, Titte, and Oppi, were to mingle with the crowd and stay near the ship.

The comedy was necessary. Since the original sacrificial victim was hidden below deck; we didn't dare leave the boat alone. Paul was part of the deception. He was only ten years old, but he was mature for his age. Sitting on the deck, he observed a small squadron of soldiers standing on the end of the pier. He held a wineskin full of sweetened wine, and he watched the soldiers pensively, waiting for the right moment to drop the wine onto the stone pier. If Plexis's scheme went as planned, the soldiers would grab it and drink, laughing and teasing the slave confined to his boat, then toss the empty wineskin back at him, jeering at Paul to tell his master he'd finished all the wine himself.

In the wine was a powerful sleeping draught. Soon after the soldiers drank it, they would fall asleep in a puzzled heap, their legs wobbling and folding under them as their minds clouded and went dark. That was when the crew would untie the boat from the pier and quietly push her out into the harbour under cover of darkness.

Axiom and Demos were drinking toasts with the guards all along the waterfront, acting the part of drunken traders delighting in the ceremonies.

Earlier, they had taken a dinghy and hidden it in a strategic spot behind a houseboat. When the time came, they would quickly row the dinghy to the sacred island, careful to avoid the sharp rocks placed around it to discourage landing.

Phaleria was plying wine on the far side of the harbour, and Plexis, the handsome prince from Athens, was right in the midst of the nobles.

It was a stroke of luck that Plexis had seen an old acquaintance. The man was amazed to see him alive – hadn't he died in Persia? He had thought he'd heard something about an incredible funeral pyre erected for Hephaestion in Babylon.

It was another Hephaestion, Plexis assured the man, and have another drink. So, you're a captain in the navy here in Carthage? How remarkable. Have another sip; the wine is excellent.

Plexis had an actor's face and voice; he soon had the crowd singing hymns to the Greek god of wine, Dionysus, while he expertly singled out the men in charge of launching the warships and gave them huge draughts of fine wine – wine laced with enough sleeping potion to have them soundly snoring just as the ceremony began.

Alexander and I had the tricky parts.

I stood next to the man whose son was about to be sacrificed in honour of Nike, goddess of victory, and I tried not to let my panic show. He was beyond noticing though. His only son was about to be burned to death; not a thing a father wants to contemplate. The poor man was so stricken that tremors shook him constantly. I was amazed he was still standing.

The roar of the crowd grew to deafening proportions as the sun set and darkness claimed the city. Torches were lit and I saw that everything would be easier than I dared hope. It was a moonless night. The water was black as jet, and a breeze made the ribbons dance. The scarlet ribbons looked black in the torchlight.

The white bull gleamed. His coat had been brushed to a satin finish, and firelight made the animal look as if he were made of gold. On his back was a slender boy. His face was a mask of terror, his eyes two huge wells of despair. His hands were tied behind his back, and two priests, walking on either side of the majestic bull, held him tightly.

At the temple, the priests pulled the boy off the bull. The youth stood, swaying, while the crowd chanted and the high priest made the necessary absolutions. Then the placid bull was led to the altar, and while a strong man held the beast's head, a priest took a golden knife and slit its throat. The bull died, a look of confusion in his great eyes, his knees buckling under him, while his steaming blood splashed into a bowl held by two priests.

The priests then poured the blood over the boy. The shock of hot blood made him scream. Next to me, his father uttered a desperate groan, and I felt a wave of icy panic wash over me.

We were standing on the beach on the right side of the sacred island. The bridge was directly behind me, it had been kept clear while the bull was led to the altar, but now the bridge was packed with the crowd, pressing as closely as the guards would allow.

In front of me was the temple, a simple sandstone building made of eight Ionic columns holding up a roof shingled with enamelled tiles. Inside the temple was the sacred altar, and beyond that was the sacrificial pyre, unlit. The temple, the dead bull, and the spectators were dappled from flickering torches. It was a scene painted black and gold, and the moving, dancing light and shadow made it hard to see things clearly. In the dimness, Alexander eased away from me and vanished into the crowd. I couldn't even pick him out. No one else would notice him either.

The priests led the boy towards the huge pile of sticks and hay. He struggled weakly in the firm grip of four priests. He was also stunned, half fainting with terror, his body covered with sticky blood. I could see where he'd wet himself in fear, the urine washing the blood away on his legs. His mouth was drawn back in dread. When I glanced at his father I saw the poor man was shaking badly. Somehow, he stayed upright as the crowd behind us pushed us towards the pyre.

I started looking for Alexander. I was also peering into the darkness, searching for a sign of our ship. Our whole plan hinged on getting away by sea. We'd been busy all day buying jars filled with crude oil and stocking them on the deck. Back then, no one really knew what to do with crude oil. It was sometimes used in lamps, but not often, because the odour was unpleasant inside a house. I knew what its characteristics were, and Alexander had thought of a way to use it in our favour. It wouldn't be long now. Priests carried torches towards the pyre, and another priest cut off locks of the boy's hair, throwing them to the four winds.

Next to me his father moaned quietly.

'Would you save your son?' I asked him in Greek.

He turned to me, his face haggard. He knew Greek. He hadn't needed Plexis to translate for him. We hadn't fallen into that trap.

75

'It is too late to do anything. The gods have chosen.'

'No, the high priest chose, but that's beside the point. I was the one who freed the other boy. Now I must save your son.' My voice was a murmur in his ear, but he heard every word.

He stiffened. 'You are too late.'

'No. Listen carefully. When the boat appears behind the temple, you must go to your son. Will you cut his bonds and free him?' This was the hardest part. The pyre would be lit. The man would have to brave a wall of flames. We counted on him to do it. A father would cross through hell to save his child, I reasoned.

He took the knife I handed him and hid it in his sleeve. Together, we moved forward. It wasn't easy, but we were amidst the nobles and the crowd wasn't as thick. Soon, we were nearly in front of the temple. On the other side of the pillars, I saw a tall man standing near of the pyre.

'Hamilcar,' breathed the man at my side.

'The war captain?'

'The man who captured Tartessos. He has come to be crowned with the laurel of victory and to partake of the wine and barley. He is the one who will light the pyre. He has known my son since he was born.'

'It won't be easy for him then,' I said.

'On the contrary. He was the one who decreed that if I couldn't find the first boy, my son was to die.' A fierce note crept into the man's voice.

In the dark, I saw Alexander. He was making his way along the boulders at the far end of the island. I hoped his plan would work. The sea breeze carried a whiff of crude oil to us. I saw several people wrinkle their noses, but the ceremony was moving towards its climax and no one turned their heads towards Alexander.

The boy's hands were bound to a post, and the priest sprinkled wine and barley over his head, chanting in a high, nasal voice. Hamilcar flung his heavy cape behind him and took off his bronze helmet. He handed it to a slave standing nearby and unclasped his sword belt, giving it to another slave.

The crowd hushed as Hamilcar approached the high priest and bowed. The priest placed a crown of laurel on the war leader's head and then offered him a chalice. Hamilcar raised it to his mouth and drank deeply. He drained the chalice, then he straightened his shoulders and took a lit torch from a slave.

He looked directly at the boy's father, then he walked towards the pyre and dipped the torch to the stack of wood. His face was impassive as he lit the fire. After the flame caught, he tossed the rest of the torch onto the pyre and stepped back.

The fire crackled. Smoke swirled up, hiding the boy from sight for a moment before the night breeze swept it away and fanned the flames to a man's height. There was a shrill scream from inside the pyre, and the boy's silhouette twisted and convulsed as he strained against the bonds that held him.

'Now!' I hissed, and gave the man a push.

I had been busy unwrapping a long rope tied around my waist. As the people stared at the fire, mesmerized, I ducked down and fastened the rope to a man's leg. The man didn't notice, too busy watching the writhing figure behind the dancing flames. I stood and made my way towards the dark shore. I wound through the crowd, holding the rope roughly knee level. In the press, no one took any notice. I worked my way from one side of the crowd to the other, making sure I passed close to the guards. I was holding my breath as I passed the rope in and out, moving as fast as I could towards Alexander, who was visible now, standing on the edge of the firelight.

Axiom and Demos were waiting in the dinghy. According to plan, our boat was now in the bay, ready to move quickly.

There came a sudden cry from the crowd as the boy's father reached the edge of the fire and plunged through, knife flashing. The surprise was so great that the priests didn't react at first. It was probably the first time that anyone had ever seen someone try to free a sacrificial victim. The boy was choking on smoke, his hair was smouldering, and his skin was blistered in places. His father didn't hesitate. He put all his weight into a mighty push that sent the boy sprawling out of the flames. The boy rolled once on the ground and Alexander was there. He picked him up and literally tossed him towards me.

I grabbed the boy and shoved him towards the rocks behind me, then handed the end of my rope to Plexis who'd surged out of the darkness. He took it and gave a mighty pull, and half the crowd in front of us fell, tangling in a thrashing melee. Hamilcar was the first to react. He snatched up his sword and leapt at Alexander. Hamilcar didn't know whom he was fighting – he had a wolfish smile on his face.

Alexander raised his sword, and there was the sudden ringing of metal against metal as the two men met at the edge of the fire. The people nearest them shrieked and scrambled out of the way, further adding to the confusion.

Plexis had the boy now, and he dunked him into the water before thrusting him into the boat. I turned towards Alexander, but Plexis caught my arm and dragged me over the boulders. He was shouting something, but I couldn't hear him; I couldn't stop screaming. The high priest had seized the boy's father and was wrestling with him. In a moment, the other priests had joined the fray, and the tussling group was heading straight for the blazing fire.

Alexander was grinning, his teeth shining in the firelight. Hamilcar was scowling, his blade flashing. However, every thrust was met with a counter thrust, and Alexander was moving like a wraith over the boulders, making his way inexorably towards us.

'Hurry!' I cried.

My voice was lost in the clamour of the crowd and the clanging of metal swords. Shrieks from people burning suddenly attracted everyone's attention. Two priests were in flames, their robes throwing sparks as they rushed about, sowing more panic in the crowd. Bystanders tried to scatter but many were tangled with my rope. More and more people fell. A woman's hair caught fire, and she started screaming. On shore, the crowd watching began to realize that something was very wrong. A low murmur was growing along the seawall like a wave rushing around it, punctuated by sharp cries.

I clambered into the dinghy and gathered the boy in my arms, holding him against my chest. He was in shock, his skin was clammy to the touch. 'Father, father,' he whispered.

'Hush, he'll be all right.' I squeezed my eyes shut. I lied. The boy's father had been forced into the pyre and was burning, his skin blackening and peeling off in layers while he screamed. There was a priest in the fire with him. Both men were locked together in a death grip. The priest uttered no sound, or maybe he was already dead.

There was a sound like a bee near my head and Plexis flung himself into the boat. 'They are shooting arrows at us,' he cried. 'Some of the guards have figured out what's going on. Stay low. We're casting off.'

'Alexander!' I screamed.

'He'll be all right.'

There was a grinding sound as the boat left the rocks, and then the boat dipped and bobbed as Axiom and Demos grabbed the oars and started to row.

'No! Alexander!' I screamed again and struggled to raise my head, but Plexis put his foot on my shoulder and shoved me to the bottom of the boat.

'Ashley, don't move!' his voice was raw.

There was a loud splashing and the boat dipped wildly again. I heard Alexander give a hoarse shout, and I felt the boat leap forward as he pushed it. Then the oars dug into the water and we rowed away. Alexander hauled himself into the boat and collapsed, dripping seawater over everything.

'Is it time? This torch is like a bull's eye to the archers,' said Demos.

'Yes!' Plexis cried.

There was an arc of sparkling light as Demos tossed the torch he held towards the shore, and a loud '*Whump!*' as the crude oil Alexander had poured on the beach and in the water caught fire. The people who'd plunged in after us screamed and tried to beat out the flames, the archers shot wide as our boat vanished into the darkness, and on the island everything was chaos.

'Are you feeling better about Tartessos now?' I asked.

Alexander didn't answer and I prodded him. 'Alex?' He didn't move, but my hand came away with something on it. I started to shake. He'd been cut; I could feel it now. Warm, sticky blood pooled in the bottom of the boat. In the dark, blindly, I felt frantically along his body with my good hand, searching for the wound. It was on his back. His tunic was sliced open and blood gushed over my fingers.

I uttered a high shriek and pushed my fist as hard as I could into the cut. Alexander moaned and I pushed harder, willing the bleeding to stop, shouting to Axiom and Demos to hurry, by the gods, to hurry.

We loaded Alexander on board first, crying to Kell that he was wounded. The tall man didn't ask questions, he grabbed Alexander and carried him below where a light could be safely lit. Demos hurried after him, shouting at Axiom to bring the medicine bag.

Plexis and I took the singed boy and pulled him aboard. Paul was waiting for us, his face strained. He'd seen his father, blood dripping from his body, being carried away. 'Is he all right?' he asked in a whisper.

I could only nod. Shock was making my teeth chatter. The boy in my arms was worse off. His skin was still cold to the touch. The deck beneath me lurched as the wind caught the sails, and we veered to the right, away from the harbour towards the open sea. Behind us were the lights of the city and the lights from the warships. Not all of them were short a captain. Some were leaving the port.

I sent Paul for a warm blanket, and we wrapped the boy in it, making a pallet for him in the shelter of the helm. Phaleria stood above us, her hair a dark cloud in the night. We were sailing blind. I hoped that Phaleria had memorized the treacherous shoreline. We headed northwest towards the mouth of a river. Phaleria was counting on the current there to give us an extra push towards the open sea. The dragon boat was one of the swiftest boats made at that time. Once out in the open, we had a good chance of outrunning the warships. However, in the bay, the low warships with three storeys of trained rowers, would catch us.

There were twenty warships fanning out to block us, the noise of their drums carrying over the sound of the waves and the faint shouts of the crowds still lined up on the waterfront.

Paul and I knelt at the boy's side, holding his hands. Another silhouette crept next to us, and I saw the other boy, the first intended victim. His name was Hirkan, and he

82

spoke to the boy in a low voice until he opened his eyes and stared up at us.

I hadn't seen his eyes until then. The night was dark, no moonlight silvered the sails or lined the hard edges of the waves, but even in the starlight I saw the clearest amber eyes staring up at me. They were more yellow than a lion's eyes, fringed with black lashes, staring out of a pale face smattered with faint freckles. His brown hair was singed, a burn marked his left cheek with an angry welt where a spark had lit upon it, and his left shoulder and leg were both burned. He looked at me and tears filled his eyes. In perfect Greek, he said, 'My father is dead, and it's all your fault.' Then he turned his head and wouldn't look at me again.

I felt as if I'd been slapped. The pain in the boy's voice had been so intense, it had struck me with the force of a blow. Paul jerked his head up and stared at me, his face frozen. He'd become good at that. His face could become as unreadable as a statue's. Alexander usually had many expressions chasing themselves across his face, and then, in an instant, he could grow still like that. Paul looked very much like his father now, staring at the wounded boy, his face in shadow.

Hirkan didn't understand Greek, but he felt what was going on between us. He leaned down and spoke to the boy, whispering harshly. At first, the boy pushed him away, rolling over on his side and curling up. However, Hirkan kept speaking in a low voice, with words as soft as the waves. He touched the boy's head now and then, prodding him gently.

I sat back and watched the dark sea around us. In a moment, we'd have to fight. The warships were not far. Arrows sometimes buzzed by like huge wasps. I wanted to go below and see how Alexander was, but my legs wouldn't carry me. I was falling apart. I had just begun to realize what I'd done beneath the blinding sun. In the split second it took to leap over a wall, I'd put us in terrible danger. I'd killed a man as surely as if I'd pushed him into the fire myself, and I'd caused Alexander to be wounded, perhaps mortally. I'd made a boy an orphan and made a mockery out of a religious ceremony that was sacred for thousands of people. I'd done it with no thought, no idea, only instinct. I'd acted as if I were alone in the world.

I stood up and walked to the stern to join Titte, Kell, and Erati. I took a jar of crude oil and stood next to them. We would pour it into the sea and set it alight. It was all we had to buy us time. We had to get to the open sea. Then, I would sit down and think of my folly. Then, I would receive the punishment I deserved.

The warships were gaining. Now the arrows fell thick and fast. One or two sliced through the sails, a few thumped into the boat's side. I felt the vibration of them as they landed. One hit the deck not two feet from where I stood. I just looked at it. Somewhere, deep inside, I wanted to be struck by an arrow. I wanted to be wounded, to be hurt, to die. I wanted to crawl into a hole and disappear. I was glad of the darkness. I wouldn't have been able to meet anyone's gaze at that moment.

Another arrow thumped into the deck. Off to starboard, a warship was dipping into the waves, her bow nearly level with ours. Axiom grunted and hurled his jar of oil into the sea, reaching down to lift another one up in a fluid motion. Next to him, Erati and Titte did the same, and I poured mine out, leaning well over the stern to do so.

Axiom caught me by the waist and pulled me back.

'No,' he said clearly. 'Sit down.' It was an order. My knees buckled and I sat down hard. Erati lit a torch and tossed it over the edge of the boat. Alexander had guessed right. The water burst into flames and the warship was engulfed in a sheet of fire.

The effect was dramatic. The other ships veered to the side, we hit the current, and soon there were five hundred metres separating us. The distance grew when we met the chop of the open sea. The warships were manoeuvrable but they were not as well rigged as the dragon boat. The wind filled our sails and the boat plunged forward like a coursing hound, spray coming over the bow.

The men standing in the back of the boat uttered a hoarse cheer, and even Phaleria gave a delighted cry. Then Demos came up the stairs, wiping his hands on his tunic. I could tell it was he. No one else had his size. Plexis was at his heels. In the dark, I couldn't see their expressions, so I didn't know how Alexander was. I was terrified, suddenly. The blood drained from my head and I hit the plank deck in the worst faint I'd ever suffered.

Chapter Six

Plexis heard me fall and was at my side in an instant. He picked me up and carried me down below, walking sure-footed as was his habit. Alexander was stretched out in his bed exhausted but alive. Demos had cauterized his wound and the smell was sickening. I didn't dare lean over him. My head was spinning and I thought I'd faint again. I knelt down next to him and took his hand. I held it to my cheek and just stayed there and shook. Then I stood again and carefully tucked the covers around him. In his drug-induced sleep, Alexander moaned. The pain would wake him in the morning.

Plexis took the lantern down and blew it out. 'Why don't you sleep,' he said gently. There was no reproach in his voice, none at all. I bowed my head and let my tears flow. In the blackness no one would see them. My pallet was made near the bed. I sat on it, too numb to undress, still shivering.

At that moment the baby in my womb moved. I felt a hard flutter then a kick. Plexis sat on the bed beside me and put his hand on the gentle swell of my belly. In the pitch darkness I leaned against him, I needed him so much; I needed his strength and his wholeness to lift me out of my melancholy.

Tears trickled down my cheeks and dripped off my chin. They landed on his hands, still clasped over my belly. Without a sound, he lay me down on my side, curling around me, lifting my tunic and running his hands up and down my body. I felt his penis stiffen as his breath grew deeper, matching my own. Hurriedly he fumbled with his own tunic, grasping my hips, pulling me to him, sheathing himself within me in one hard thrust. Battle did that to people, the aftermath left them taut as strung bows.

For a moment he didn't move, I could feel him trying to regain control, but the boat rocked us, I was as slippery as only a fully aroused woman can be, and with a groan he bucked into me, his fingers digging into my hips as he pulled and thrust.

I uttered a soft moan, feeling my whole body dissolve into a boneless shiver of delight. The throbbing that shook me came from within and from Plexis too. He jerked helplessly, caught in the throes of passion, spending himself with a groan that echoed my own.

Afterwards, I drifted to sleep, Plexis still clasping me in his arms. The boat rocked and rocked, the night was still young, and we had far to go before we were safe.

We were heading towards the surest safety we knew, Rome, mortal enemy of Carthage. On deck was the boy whose descendant would bring about her downfall. Scipio Atticus. I had recognized the name. Scipio was the name of the man who would fight Hannibal and defeat Carthage.

I was tried, found guilty, and hung from the yardarm, the rope digging into my flesh, choking me. I kicked and struggled, my life flashing before my eyes. Below me, the people whose lives I'd endangered looked on with flat stares. Their faces were marble, their eyes slate. I couldn't speak; the rope was too tight. I was strangling.

'Ashley, Ashley, hush, it's just a dream.' Plexis was leaning over me, his eyes full of worry. 'You have a fever, that's all. It's all right.'

'Where am I?' I blinked and looked around. My head pained me; my throat was dry and hurt abominably. The light stabbed my eyes and I closed them. I was lying in a bed, on the ship, in a small space between a large crate of resin and bales of hay. Plexis was kneeling by my side, a damp cloth in his hand. He was gently smoothing it over my forehead. 'What happened?' I asked.

'We escaped from Carthage. The boys are safe, Alexander is fine, just very tired now, and you became feverish and slept for nearly two days. You've been delirious, talking in your own language, frightening the crew.'

'I'm sorry,' I croaked.

Plexis raised my head and gave me some water. 'I've been so worried,' he said, and I saw it was true. His eyes were ringed with dark circles and his face was drawn.

'I'm so sorry,' I repeated, feeling my throat tighten. 'Is everyone furious with me? Will they ever forgive me?'

'Forgive you? For what?'

'For causing so much death and destruction, for endangering everyone's lives, for getting us into such a mess, and for killing Scipio's father. I'll never forgive myself. That poor boy, I killed his father.'

'What are you talking about?' Plexis sounded truly perplexed. He put his hand on my forehead and frowned. 'The fever's almost gone, but you're still raving.'

'No I'm not. We were almost killed by my folly.'

Plexis sat back and put his chin in his hands. He studied me for a while. Finally he sighed and dipped his cloth in some water again and wiped off my face, tenderly, gently. 'Ashley, oh, Ashley. Why do you insist on taking the blame for everything? All right, I know you feel responsible; after all, if you hadn't saved Hirkan, Scipio would never have been sacrificed. But what do you think Hirkan feels about all this? Doesn't he have some say in the matter? Scipio has had time to reflect, and although he still grieves for his father, he realizes that his death was unavoidable. Someone had to die. And he realizes that his father preferred to give his life so that he could live.'

'Stop it, you're starting to sound like a lawyer again.'

'I am a lawyer. All right. The truth is Scipio is still very upset. So are we all. Alexander is still very weak, and he'll probably never move his shoulder as well as he used to. Demos and Phaleria are upset because they lost most of their precious wine store, and Titte, Kell, and Oppe are muttering about the tears in the sails where the arrows ripped through them. Erati will probably never get over losing his clay oven. That is, until we buy him a new one. Paul has worried himself sick about you, and Yovanix can hardly comfort him. Axiom had to use up all the alum in the medical bag to heal Alexander, and he's worried about your fever. Therefore, in all honesty, I suppose you are rather an unpopular person today. But tomorrow things will look better, and you'll see that everything that happened was just as much our fault as anyone else's.'

'What do you mean?'

'Well, there was a hundred talent reward for the return of the slave. Phaleria and Demos could have cashed in any time they liked. Instead they proposed using their wine, and Axiom was the one who thought up the scheme of doctoring it. Alexander was spoiling for a good fight; he has been for months. He was thrilled to heft his sword and fight against a real swordsman like Hamilcar, whom he killed, by the way. He's sleeping with a huge grin on his face. Erati dragged his clay oven to the stern to light the oil, and he was the one who stepped on it and broke it. He says he was startled by the sight of flames on top of the water. He also says he wouldn't have missed it for the world. Moreover, Oppi, Titte, and Kell really have nothing better to do today than to mend sails. So you see, everyone will get over their fright and forgive you, if they ever blamed you in the first place, which I sincerely doubt.'

'What about Scipio?' I asked in a low voice.

Plexis paused. 'Well, I suppose we'll just have to let time take its course. He seems to get on very well with Paul and Hirkan. They stay together. The three boys are almost the same age. Paul is the youngest, I think, but easily the tallest.' His voice was proud. He loved Paul as if he were his own son. Plexis gave me a soft kiss on the cheek and disappeared. I closed my eyes. The baby in my belly gave a fluttering kick and I smiled.

I must have slept for a while. When I awoke, I felt better and wanted to go up on deck, but the weather had taken a turn for the worse and almost everyone was down below. Plexis sat in his corner with his mending. Axiom was reorganizing the medical bag, making a list of all that we needed. Phaleria and Demos were making love in the far corner, hidden by curtains and out of sight, though not of sound. Their sighs and whispers merged with the patter of rain on the deck and the gusts of wind in the sails.

Alexander was lying very still, reading a scroll. His back was stiff, but healing better than he'd thought it would. Yovanix was whittling, his deft hands carving a smooth bowl from a knotty piece of black wood. The two boys we'd rescued were playing dominos, the click, clicking of the bones a gentle counterpoint to the sighs of the wind.

'Do you want an infusion?' Paul asked me, a bowl of steaming chamomile in his hands.

I nodded gratefully and sat up straighter. My headache was gone but my throat still hurt. I sipped the hot drink and smiled at my son.

'Erati made a whole pot of it, there's lots more. I had some earlier.' His voice was low. The boat dipped into a swell and I held the bowl away from me, careful not to spill it.

Alexander shifted in his bed and reached for the vial of mint drops the druid had made for him. His seasickness was held in check. He always smelled of fresh mint on board.

Paul looked at me gravely. 'Plexis said you were sad,' he said.

I nodded. 'I was. However, I feel much better now. I only wish ...'

'Wish what?'

'That Scipio would speak to me. I feel so awful about what happened to his father. Do you think he'll ever forgive me?'

Paul smiled tenderly. 'Don't worry, he's starting to see that what happened wasn't all your fault. I think he's even angrier at Father.'

'At Alexander? But, why?'

'Because he killed Hamilcar, and Scipio wanted to do it himself when he grew older. He's sworn eternal vengeance against Hamilcar's whole family.'

'He has?' I sat up even straighter and frowned.

'Prince Hamilcar is dead, but he has a son, also called Hamilcar, and Scipio will not rest until the whole family is destroyed.'

'But why?'

'Because, well, I'm sure he can explain it better than I can. Wait a minute, I'll fetch him.' He was up in a fluid motion, before I could wave him back. Then he returned, Scipio behind him, his face set in hard lines, his golden eyes flashing.

'My Lady,' he said, bowing shortly before he sat down next to me.

I shook my head. 'I'm not your lady. I'm Ashley, that's all. I wanted to tell you how very sorry I am your father lost his life. If I'd known what was going to happen, I would have ... I'd have ...' I stopped, flustered. Actually, I had no idea what I would have done. *Let Hirkan be killed* sounded terrible. Besides, I didn't mean it. 'I'm sorry,' I said inanely, wishing there was something – anything – I could say.

He seemed to understand. A sad smile twisted his features. 'I'm sorry too, Lady Ashley. However, let us not dwell upon it. Tonight we will sacrifice a lamb to the gods and pray to Hermes to lead my father's shade to the underworld. He had no money in his mouth, so perhaps a prayer to the ferryman to take him across the river Styx.'

I nodded. 'What will you do now?'

'I have family in Rome; my father's sister married a senator.'

'I'm so sorry,' I whispered again.

'I have decided to forgive you,' he said evenly. 'I am thirteen years old now, old enough to understand that what happened was written by the gods themselves. Now I have but one goal in life, to destroy Hamilcar's descendants.'

'I don't understand,' I said shaking my head. 'Paul told me you'd explain.'

'Hamilcar has been looking for an excuse to destroy my father for years. They were old enemies, at odds about many things, but most of all about Tartessos. My father was a peace-loving man; he never wanted Carthage to go to war. He said that the city's greatness could come from trade, not war. Hamilcar did not agree. My father had the king's ear. Now that our family has been eradicated, I suppose that the Barcas will rise to certain power. Hamilcar's son is called Barca. He is but a babe, but I will make sure my own sons know who he is, and someday, if the gods will it, my father will be avenged.' He raised his hands, palms upwards, towards the sky. His face was tense. His words had all the weight of his pain behind them. I didn't doubt for an instant that he would succeed.

'What is your uncle's name?' I asked.

'Augustus.' A clap of thunder startled us. The sky was black now.

Kell poked his head down the stairway and called to us to make sure everything was securely fastened. 'A storm is rising,' he said.

I nodded. *A storm indeed.* I looked pensively at the boy sitting cross-legged in front of me. His golden eyes were uncanny in their intensity. His grandson would bring about the downfall of a fabled city.

The gods were roaring in the sky. Thunder boomed and lightning tore the sky apart with the sound of the heavens being ripped wide open. The boat heeled and dived into a trough and everyone gasped. Only I smiled. The storm would not sink the ship. I was staring at a golden-eyed boy, and suddenly the words of Apollo came back to me. I laughed then softly. Perhaps it really was true. Mine was not the power to change anything. But those around me would change everything.

The storm blew over quickly, leaving a glassy calm in its wake. The sun set on a sea as flat as a mirror and we ate dinner on deck, sitting on damp wood, admiring the reds and oranges of the variegated sky. Alexander was moving about now, holding himself carefully, his face chalky. I had ceased to worry about him though. He'd been wounded before and knew what to do when he was injured. We weren't at war any more; he didn't need to drive himself.

He took a bowl of fish stew from Erati and sat down by my side, grunting a little with the effort of moving.

'Better?' he asked me.

'Much, thank you, what about yourself?'

'I'll be all right in a day or two. Or maybe three.' He wriggled his shoulder and winced. 'The sword cut the muscle, luckily it went with the fibre and not against it. It will fully recover, unlike my leg.' He stuck the offending member out and moved his foot to illustrate its limited range of movement. His fibula had been shattered and he still limped. I knew how vain he was, so I refrained from saying anything. He sighed and crossed his legs again, holding his steaming bowl on his lap.

Alexander had wanted to be a doctor; he had begged his father to let him study on Kos, an island where there was a famous medical school. However, his father had sent him to Aristotle, and the result was sitting next to me, eating his fish stew, for all the world like a common mortal.

I grinned, suddenly euphoric. The breeze ruffled the water, and the sails bellied out gently, moving the boat smoothly through the glassy sea. I felt as if the naiads themselves were pushing our boat along, as if the sun were really Helios driving his chariot across the path of the heavens, and as if Poseidon were watching over us, making sure the voyage was swift and safe.

Alexander stopped eating and peered at me. 'How much wine did you have?' he asked, his mouth quirking.

I shook my head. 'None. I'm just happy, that's all. Happier than I've been in months, happier than I've been in years!' I laughed then, out of sheer joy. 'I can't believe it. I feel, I don't know, free somehow. As if everything has suddenly fallen into place and the world is exactly as it should be. I feel as if heavy chains have fallen off my shoulders and the future is as golden as the horizon. Look at that sunset, isn't it incredible?'

Alexander smiled, his eyes glittering suddenly. 'You always could surprise me,' he said softly, and he kissed me.

I closed my eyes, melting into his kiss, letting his lips roam softly over mine. He broke off and I sighed.

'I feel as if everything has been resolved. It's strange. Babylon has ceased to haunt me. Strange, and wonderful at the same time. I no longer fear for Paul. Your soul has been returned, and I don't mourn my missing hand any more. I am looking forward to seeing Rome, Pompeii, and then going home to Alexandria. I feel in my heart that Africa is my home, and I long to go back to our house on the hill and give birth to this child.' I put my hand on my belly and smiled down at it.

Alexander nodded. 'I too feel as if we've passed a certain point, as if we have been climbing a mountain and suddenly find ourselves on the summit.'

'That's exactly what I mean,' I said. 'But does it mean that everything else will be downhill from now on? An anticlimax, as it were?'

'No, I think not. There are other mountains and valleys before us. The valleys may be green and fertile, the mountains steep. But whatever they may be we will cross them together, and that makes all the difference, doesn't it?'

'Your lips are the headiest wine I know,' I said, smiling brilliantly at my husband, running a hand through his hair. 'Look, a white hair. Soon you will be venerable.'

'A venerable old man?' he wrinkled his nose. 'I don't think I ever expected to become one of those.'

'You'll make a wonderful grandfather,' I teased. 'I can see you now, sitting beneath the olive trees, a sprig of basil tucked behind your ear, a grandchild sitting on your lap begging you to tell him about the time you went to India.'

'And about the time we floated underwater, remember? In the glass bell?'

'And when we saw the tiger. It was magnificent, wasn't it?'

He nodded, sipping his soup thoughtfully. 'I wonder sometimes if I'll go back. I think I'd like to, someday. I'll tell you something else. I don't see myself spending the rest of my days in Alexandria. A year perhaps, but no more. After that, I see us travelling again. I hope it will be with Nearchus, perhaps to the lands behind Egypt. Perhaps back to India or to China. Perhaps, who knows, towards the new lands you showed me on your map of the world? However, in the end, I think I'd like to go the valley of Nysa, the Sacred Valley, and grow old there. If there is a paradise on earth, I think it's by a silver lake under the apricot trees.'

Chapter Seven

We arrived in the harbour just outside Rome and docked the boat after going through customs and carefully filling out several clay tablets, a wax tablet, and five long sheets of papyrus. We had to write out everything that was in the boat, as well as our names and the reason for our visit. After passing customs, we sailed the ship down the river and found a berth in the city. The dock area was vast and located on a curve of the river. Once we'd disembarked, we were shown to a customs building to fill out more documents.

The Roman official sitting behind a desk looked like a modern bureaucrat, except for the statues of the gods carefully lined up on a low shelf behind him and the feathered helmet he wore. He frowned over the documents we'd completed, asked a few questions, and then bade us welcome to Rome. Just before we walked out the door, he told us that there were a few little rules we had to follow while in the city, that we'd find a stack of papyrus by the exit, and to take one and study it carefully.

We picked up a copy of the rules and stared at the long list. It went like this – but I have left out quite a few for lack of space:

First rule: No pissing in the streets. Public toilets are located at certain corners. You can ask a Roman citizen to direct you.

Second rule: Roman gods are to be honoured above all others.

Third rule: The public baths are for Roman citizens only. Anyone else must get a guest pass.

Fourth rule: Slaves must be inside by sunset. Any slave on the streets after the sun sets must have a special pass.

Fifth rule: No writing on the walls – this rule was widely ignored; graffiti was everywhere, but if you got caught you paid a fine.

Sixth rule: No animals except dogs, birds, cats, and monkeys are allowed in the city. No lions, cheetahs, wolves, or snakes, even on leashes. For horses, goats, and cattle see rule twenty-three.

Seventh rule: Drive chariots and wagons on the left side of the street. Cross streets on the raised crossings. Don't block traffic. Don't walk in the middle of the road. Stay on the sidewalks. The pedestrian streets are forbidden to wheeled vehicles during the day. See the section in the rules marked 'vehicles'.

Eighth rule: Roman citizens have the first choice of seats in the stadium. Tickets can be procured for guests at the east gate.

Ninth rule: Keep your guest pass and identification with you at all times.

Tenth rule: No littering. Garbage bins are at every street corner.

Eleventh, twelfth, and thirteenth rules: No spitting in the streets. No nudity in the streets. No swearing at the policemen.

The rest of the rules were mainly along the same lines. No this, no that. Rome was a small city at the time, but an extremely bossy and well-organized one. There were police everywhere, and Roman citizens were most helpful about explaining things.

The poorer people lived in apartments or in cramped houses in the suburbs, while the richer folk lived outside the city in vast estates. Slaves made up a good part of the population, though perhaps not as large as in Athens. Slaves were also less respected here, the Romans tended towards snobbery. I noticed that there were many three and four-storey apartment buildings, quite a large suburban development, and a very beautiful city centre. The roofs were shingled with red tiles, the buildings were made of brick and stone covered with whitewash, and everywhere you looked were cunning gardens and temples.

At first we were silent, walking on the left side of the street and being careful not to pee, swear, or spit. Scipio was taking us to his uncle's house. He had been there once before so he was fairly sure where to go. Just to make sure, we stopped and asked a Roman citizen the way, showing him the address and trying not to look too much like tourists.

We couldn't help staring though. Even Alexander was affected, although he was trying very hard not to show it. He'd somehow decided he didn't like Romans. Was it jealousy? Roman men were tall, dark, and handsome.

Roman citizens walked with a swagger, sure that their city, their togas, and their ... well, their everything was vastly superior than anything else in the world at that time.

I was dazzled. Even the ancient cities of Babylon and Taxila looked worn around the edges compared to the new splendour of Rome. Because, compared to the older Persian and Greek cities, it was brand-new.

Imagine, Memphis was founded in 2990 BC, more than twenty-five centuries before Rome! Babylon, the queen of cities, was raised to her position of capital of Mesopotamia under Nebuchadnezzar in 1124 BC, nearly a thousand years before Rome was even founded. Those cities were built of sun-baked brick and mud, and as you know, rain, wind, and snow have a habit of weathering dried mud no matter how lovely it is. When I saw Babylon, most of the buildings had been rebuilt at least twenty times. The ziggurat was under constant repair, and the palace always had a wall to shore up, tiles on the roof to replace, paint to freshen, and although these tasks were carried out immediately, the city still looked, well, ancient.

'It's not that amazing,' sniffed Plexis, as we stepped out of the customs offices. He shrugged at the gate and the wall to the city. 'A whole city built of volcanic stone. It's very grey and dreary.' But his jaw dropped when we rounded the corner leading to the Circus Maximus, the biggest sports arena in the world at that time. On Capitoline Hill there was the temple Jupiter Optimus Maximus, where Juno, Minerva, and Jupiter were worshipped. It was huge. 'What are all those geese doing there?' Plexis pointed to a huge flock of grey, brown, and white geese that appeared to be nesting on the steps of the temple.

'Those are the sacred geese of Juno, and they alerted the soldiers guarding Rome when barbarians tried to creep up on them,' I said, remembering my history lessons.

'A flock of geese is called a gaggle,' said Alexander, taking my elbow. 'Careful, the path is steep here. I like how they've used the hills to fortify the city. When you're at the bottom, you can't tell what's on the other side. If I were going to attack …'

'No drawing up battle plans,' I said, shaking my head. 'Instead, look at how cleverly they've used cement to make these tall buildings. They press stones or bricks into the wet cement for decoration.'

The men were suitably impressed. I noticed that Alexander was standing up very straight, walking with his military step, and that Plexis had adjusted his cloak to hide the mended part. Axiom kept stopping to gape, which made Alexander bump into him once – they were both staring at the palace – which made Alexander very cross. We felt like country bumpkins, but not for long. It was Axiom who pointed out the graffiti on the walls. A lot of it was about Alexander and his conquests, most of it very flattering, and he soon regained his confidence.

We had arrived in the city at the same time as the salt gatherers were leaving to go to the salt flats, part of Rome's most important riches. The men were walking to work; their long wooden rakes balanced on their shoulders, empty baskets dangling from their hands. They would return by sunset to sell their salt at the salt market, held in the cool of the evening at the central marketplace.

The sun warmed the brick walls of the town, and the streets became crowded. The early morning market was over, mid-morning was the time for business and work. Important-looking men strode through the streets, bodyguards clearing the way for them. A couple times we saw chariots with drivers and their passengers, but most people walked. On every street, slaves worked very hard cleaning the gutters and walls, cooking, painting, fetching, and whatever slaves did to stay useful.

In the bustling streets, women chatted and gossiped. Most held baskets to carry their shopping, and some had children, attached to short leashes. One or two had dogs, also on leashes, and a few women had slaves or servants with them. In contrast with the Celtic women, those of Rome wore simple, almost drab clothing.

As we walked, I became interested in the hundreds of plaques encrusted in nearly every wall. They were put up to commemorate an event, and the Romans loved an 'event'; everything was an excuse for a new engraved plaque. For example, on the Forum wall I found an inscription to Romulus. I was forever pausing to read the inscriptions, and Alexander was obliged to drag me along after him, telling me I'd have plenty of time to sightsee another day.

Scipio's uncle lived on the outskirts of Rome, so we took the north road past the Quirinal hill outside the walls of Rome into the countryside. We skirted the farmer's market, following the directions a haughty Roman citizen had given us.

We arrived shortly after noon, the hot sun beating upon our heads, our legs weary from walking on the – albeit excellent – roads. All the roads were carefully paved with smooth, flat rocks. They were wide and straight, with benches beneath shady trees. Another plus were the clearly marked fountains and signs everywhere. The only dusty part had been a short detour around a section of road under repair.

We arrived in front of a lavish gate with the inscription "GENVS AVGVSTVS" carved in a plaque of hard black marble. The gate was similar to the ones we'd seen in Gaul; it had two stone pillars, a stone cattle guard, and a wrought-iron door. We entered through a small door on the side, leaving the one for chariots and wagons closed. A slave was at the entrance, opening and closing everything. He was a young boy, about ten years old, and he fell into step beside us, asking our names and the reason for our visit. When he'd memorized everyone's name, he sprinted ahead down the long, cypress-lined driveway to announce us.

As we arrived, a slender woman stepped onto the porch and held her arms out dramatically.

'Scipio! Scipio!' she called, 'Oh, my darling nephew!'

We stood back and let the boy greet his family. He wept in his aunt's arms and then wiped his face and shook hands bravely with his uncle. I let my eyes wander around the front yard. It was very beautiful, shaded by old walnut trees with cypress and laurel hedges delineating the different gardens.

There was a circular terrace laid out with large paving stones, with a fountain and fishpond in the centre. Benches were placed in the shade of a willow tree. Laurel hedges then curved around a rose garden before becoming straight again and leading off towards the stables. At the stables I caught a glimpse of a slave leading four horses to a large stone watering trough. Another slave was sweeping a path paved in round bricks, and I wondered how many workers it took to keep the place up. The hedges were all perfectly clipped and everything was clean and shiny, especially the inside of the Roman's house.

'It's just a small property, really,' said Scipio's uncle modestly. 'I have a greater estate in Gaul, looked after by my overseer. We go there during the summer months when it gets too hot here.'

I sipped my watered wine while I admired the painted walls and tiled floors. The furniture was comfortable, and it was nice to be sitting after our long walk.

'You came from the docks by foot? My poor boy! So tell me everything. News came only yesterday of your father's death. Carthage has declared war on Rome, nothing new I assure you. The Senate will meet later today and we'll decide what to do; a diplomat or two should smooth over the problem.' Scipio's uncle, Augustus, smiled at us. He was a tall, handsome man, sure of his estate, his power, and his wealth.

Scipio's aunt, named Elaina, sat on a low chair and dabbed at her eyes. She had cried bitterly at the news of her brother's death, and she swore to Scipio that she would take care of him and love him like a mother. She was theatrical, but she was a striking woman with golden eyes and jet-black hair. She was dressed in a simple but lovely robe made of fine silvery-grey linen, and she wore a necklace that any museum in the world would give millions to own. It was made of emeralds and rubies, set with intricately carved gold beads. Every now and then she would reach up and touch it lightly, as if to reassure herself it was still there.

'Dry your tears, wife,' said Augustus to Elaina. 'Since the gods did not bless us with children, we will adopt your brother's son. My nephew Scipio will be my legal heir.'

Scipio wiped the tears off his face. 'I am honoured, Uncle. I swear to bring only honour to your name.'

'A blessing upon us!' cried Elaina. 'Bring wine, that we may celebrate. We will mourn later, when the proper sacrifices have been made. We cannot have a procession or cremation, but we will commemorate him during the Parentalia. Did anyone catch his last breath?'

'No,' Scipio replied, new tears welling in his eyes.

'What is the Parentalia? I asked.

'A holiday to honour the family's ancestors. We have it in the winter, and in the spring we appease their ghosts with another ceremony.' Augustus gave me a bemused look. 'Where are you from? You speak Latin well, but your accent is a strange one.'

'I'm from …' I stopped, unsure what to say.

Alexander said, 'She comes from the far north. Ah, here is the wine. Shall we drink a toast to Scipio's new family?'

We drank a toast to Scipio, to his father, to his new parents, and then we were free to do as we pleased. Rooms were being prepared for us and lunch would be served on the back terrace. I staggered off to find a bath. I was more than a little drunk; all those toasts on very little breakfast were making my head swim.

I was glad to sink into a large marble tub filled with warm water and soak for a while. I was even happier to find shampoo and soap from Gaul, and when I was through bathing and dressed in clean robes, I felt sober again. Then a bronze bell was rung from somewhere deep in the house, and slaves came to lead us to lunch. I made sure Paul's tunic was clean, that he'd washed his face and hands and behind his ears. Then I gave him a kiss and we descended the wooden stairs together.

A tall pine tree cast blue shade onto the terrace where we were seated on comfortable chairs in front of a table covered with incredible mosaics. First, plates of fresh anchovies marinated in oil and a stuffed sow's vulva were passed around. I ate some of the former. I didn't even try a bite of the latter. A whole carp was presented afterwards. It had been cooked, cooled, and set in clear aspic surrounded by watercress and slices of apple. We ate it cold, with various spicy sauces. For dessert, we were treated to almonds dipped in salt and honey and freshly sliced melon with cardamom seeds. I admired the glassware – Phoenician – and the knives – from Gaul.

The Romans, as I soon discovered, had the weirdest food I'd ever eaten. They ate things that would make a Persian cringe – and Persians would eat just about anything. Romans mixed honey or salt in unexpected ways, serving sweetened meat, salted wine, bread stuffed with herbs, and birds stuffed with fish. Eels were a favourite addition – they were served with just about anything, the result being a rather strong, fishy taste to many dishes.

The Romans knew how to live. They adored their comfort, and I had yet to find a –wealthy – Roman's house that didn't have central heating, toilets, and running water. Plebeians had a simpler life. They lived in buildings that were often heated with bronze braziers. However, most of them did have running water, thanks to water towers. The city dwellers lived in apartment buildings often five stories high. They had to descend into the streets to fetch water.

Mindful of the stories that I'd heard about lead poisoning, I relied on spring water to quench my thirst, and there were many springs and spring-fed fountains. The city of Rome believed bread should be free to the poor. They could go to a special bakery and serve themselves. They even had something like food stamps, enabling them to buy food for their children too. As did Athens, Rome took care of her citizens.

Right after lunch, Augustus went to Rome. He stood in a chariot pulled by two black horses and driven by a Macedonian slave named Polliana. Polliana was a man, despite the name, and he was thrilled to find Alexander was from Macedonia. He spoke of Iskander the Great Conqueror in such glowing terms that Alexander was quite taken with him, even whispering to me that he was thinking about buying his freedom from Augustus. I was all for it, the fewer slaves the better, in my opinion, but the ever-practical Plexis wanted to know if Polliana would still be able to keep his job with Augustus, and if we really needed a chariot driver right now.

'We don't have a chariot for him to drive, and we don't have the money to buy him anyway,' I said. 'Our resources are dwindling rapidly. Pretty soon we'll be begging on the street.'

'You can beg,' said Plexis, pointing at my hand. 'Just take that off and hook a basket over your arm. Try to look pitiful. The pregnancy will help – people are suckers for poor widows.'

'Very funny.' I scowled, then gave a sigh. 'I miss our house on the hill. I didn't think I'd ever get used to living anywhere but a tent, but I loved Alexandria. When do you think we'll be back?'

'I heard from Ptolemy, he's moved the seat of his government to Alexandria. It won't be easy living there. I'm thinking we'll have to settle somewhere else. Why not here in Rome?' Alexander asked.

I blinked. The idea that we could settle somewhere other than Alexandria hadn't crossed my mind. But why not? Rome seemed a civilized place. 'We still need money', I said.

'I'll send a message to Ptolemy. He'll send funds to Pompeii, which is where we're headed next. We'll have to go to Alexandria anyhow to fetch the children and settle our business there. I wonder how Usse will feel about moving with us to Rome? And Brazza too. I hope they'll stay with us. We'll have to get a big house – with stables – I didn't forget you, Plexis. Oh, and then we can buy Polliana.' Alexander had a one track mind.

Chapter Eight

We borrowed Polliana and one of Augustus's chariots and went to Rome again next day. Plexis, Alexander, Axiom, and I were eager to go, but Paul wanted to stay with his new friends. I insisted he accompany us, figuring it would be a good chance for him to get a 'future' lesson, and for me to see the splendour of Rome while it was still untarnished or jammed with hover cars and tourists.

Well, there were no hover cars, of course, but there were tourists. Barbarians came from all over to see Rome, although it pained Alexander, and especially Plexis, to hear themselves referred to as 'barbarians'.

'Roman citizens in this line, barbarians over there,' called out a man in a strong voice as we lined up to buy tickets to the show at the circus.

'Barbarian? I'm Greek,' sputtered Plexis.

'And I'm —' He got no further. I clapped my hand over Alexander's mouth.

'We want to *see* the show, not star in it,' I said, shaking my head and whispering fiercely. 'Can you imagine what would happen if anyone got wind of who you were? How much do you think you're worth? Don't you know there are some who would pay a fortune to see you in the arena? It's

110

big business here. So don't, I beg of you, don't breathe a word to anyone about your identity.'

'What about the papers we filled out in the customs building?' he asked, a glint in his blue eye.

'No one ever reads official documents. They just get stored. The only ones who'll ever read them are archaeologists who will find them thousands of years from now. Now get into the barbarian line and be quiet.'

Plexis bit back a laugh as Alexander glared at him, but the glare lacked conviction, and I thought he was strangely quiet for the remainder of the afternoon.

'What do you suppose he's thinking?' I asked Plexis, drawing him aside as we toured the palace behind a group of Egyptians, two large, hairy Gauls, and a rowdy bunch of Iberians.

'I don't know, but I heard him muttering, "barbarian indeed" a couple times. I don't like the look in his eyes.' Plexis whispered back. 'Wow, did you see that staircase? A whole regiment could march down it abreast. I think the statues are creepy, especially the eyes. In Greece we don't make them look so life-like. Granted, we paint the robes, but we don't do eyes like that.' Plexis leaned towards a statue and would have touched it, but the tour guide barked at him and he drew back.

'I hope Alexander's not going to do anything foolish,' I said to Plexis worriedly. 'He *is* acting strangely.'

He was unnaturally silent, preoccupied, with his head tilted and a faraway look in his eyes. He used to look like that when I first met him. When he was in the midst of battle plans against his biggest enemy, Darius, or when he was dreaming up some impossible scheme. Although, to do him credit, it usually worked. He was probably imagining ways to conquer the city. Good thing he didn't have his army with him. I sighed and turned to Paul. 'What do you think of Rome?' I asked.

'Amazing,' he said, 'really eely.'

'Really eely"?' I asked.

'It means "great". Everyone says that,' he explained. 'Scipio's cousins told us.'

'Maybe they were just teasing,' I said. But then again, young people always had their own slang, even in these times. *Really eely?*

We passed a gymnasium where women in bikinis were exercising. The women were just visible if you peered through the arched doorways. The bikinis they wore were interesting, made of what looked like suede or knitted material. The women were jumping rope, playing with a large inflated ball, or jumping in unison in an aerobics class. Afterwards, they could swim in the heated pool inside the gymnasium. There was a women's side and a men's side. I wanted a glimpse of the men, but Alexander took my arm and pulled me away.

'We're losing the tour group,' he said.

'It's a very nice city,' I remarked for the hundredth time, strolling up the Cardo, the main street, which ran north to south. It was perpendicular to the second main street of Rome, called the Decumanus, running east to west. All the streets were parallel to either of these two streets, creating perfectly square or rectangular tenement blocks, called *insulae*. It was hilly, and we hiked up and down, with alternating views of the river and city.

'Not as nice as Alexandria,' he said with a shrug. 'But I think I could get used to living here.'

I looked at him but he was busy measuring the width of the street with his eyes, taking in the pedestrian crossings and the garbage bin placed in the alley. 'Too many policemen,' he said, shaking his head. 'They are everywhere.'

'Waiting to catch someone pissing, swearing, or spitting so they can fine them,' I said.

'I suppose they need funds to pay those policemen. I wonder if they have quotas,' Alexander said.

'I think it's a pity everything nice is reserved for Roman citizens. Even the nicest hotels. Alexandria is much more democratic,' I said.

'I wonder how long that will last. Ptolemy is a snob.'

Alexander stopped speaking for a while, and we wandered after the group listening to the guide as he spoke about the wonders of Rome. Paul and Axiom were paying close attention, Plexis was looking in the boutiques, and the Iberians started to sing a loud song. A policeman strode towards them with a determined look on his face and a wax tablet in his hands.

'No singing unless it's praise for the Roman gods,' he said sternly. 'Rule number sixteen. If you continue you'll be fined three sesterces.'

The Iberians were outraged; they'd been singing a song about good food and wine, and a very fine song it was indeed. However the policeman wouldn't budge, so they reluctantly quieted down and went on their way, until one of them got the idea of replacing the food with the names of the Roman gods. They started again, braying all about delicious Juno, spicy Venus, and hot and tasty Minerva, which made more than one Roman turn and stare.

Alexander grinned and then sighed again. He looked almost melancholy.

'What is it?' I asked him.

'I'm still not used to being a tourist. You were right when you told me I had to learn to let the world turn without me pushing it along. I keep thinking there is something I have to do or people I have to see. Don't worry. I'll get over it.'

The Iberians were now kicking in rhythm, narrowly missing a matron out walking her dog. The dog barked frantically, yap-yapping as little dogs tend to do.

The Iberians stopped and stared. Small dogs were not common in Iberia.

'What is this?' asked one, bending over and peering at the curly-haired pet. To get a better look, he reached down and picked up the dog by its tail, making it screech.

The others gathered around, ignoring the fuss the woman was making. 'Put my Popsia down right now!' she ordered, waving her arms.

'What is a "Popsia"? Is it a cat?' asked one of the big men.

'What can it be? It's quite unique! Look, all those curls! Where did you find it?' asked another Iberian to the Roman woman.

The woman snatched her dog out of his hands and hurried down the street, muttering angrily about barbarians and how Rome was going to come to a bad end if they didn't crush them all now, immediately, before they overran the city completely. 'Get civilized!' was her parting shot to the bemused Iberians.

The tour guide came back to get the Iberians, hastily explaining to them that small dogs were cherished pets and that they were not to bother them in the future.

'Is it in the rules?' asked the tallest Iberian, the one who'd started singing. 'Rule number thirty-six. No holding cherished pets by their tails on public streets!' He mimicked the policeman perfectly, causing his friends to howl in delight.

The tour guide started to get a haunted look.

Plexis and Axiom were waiting impatiently with the Egyptians, the Gauls having abandoned the tour to find something for lunch. Paul, Alexander, and I were standing nearby, watching the antics of the Iberians and wondering who would get fined first. Alexander wanted to bet, making me retort that he was getting as bad as the Roman soldiers. Paul giggled and said he was betting on the tall fellow, and father and son put their heads together to decide how much they would bet, and what the loser would have to do.

We set out again, Plexis and Axiom listening carefully to the guide, the Egyptians walking in single file and not making any comments about anything, then the Iberians, Paul and Alexander, and me, bringing up the rear. I was content to walk slowly, savouring the sights and smells, listening sometimes to the guide and sometimes to the

Iberians. They were wondering where they could get a good dinner and asked the guide to recommend a restaurant. We were not far from a small bar, called a *thermopolium*, which sold cups of wine and pickled fish and eels. There were also different sorts of bread, some cheese, and a choice of fresh fruit. We elected to stop and have lunch, and so we ate, standing at the counter.

That was my introduction to Rome, and I thought I could get to like it. The city was clean and spacious, the citizens on the whole were pleasant, and the food was, well, interesting.

We left the guide to his Iberians and made our way to the docks. We'd seen enough for one morning. Axiom took leave of us; he was going to return to the villa. Before we'd left, Elenia had asked him to stop at the sandal-maker and pick up a pair of fine leather shoes she'd ordered. I looked at the shoes. They had two-inch heels, pointed toes, and pretty laces. I compared them to my flat, uninteresting sandals, and immediately made plans to spend money on new shoes. Shoes were *the* fashion accessory in ancient Greece and Rome; styles changed constantly. I had always preferred the practical to the fashionable, but that was when I was walking twenty kilometres a day with the army. Now I could find something that flattered my feet.

When we arrived at the river, we found a crowd gathered around the dragon boat. Phaleria had started trading at the docks. She would continue trading for the next few days, taking her goods to the various marketplaces around the city. Erati had gone off in search of supplies, and Oppe and Kell had gone with him, leaving Vix and Demos to help Phaleria. Yovanix sat on a stool, whittling something from a piece of hardwood, the dog Perilous at his feet. Paul went to him and started telling him all about the sights we'd seen, describing it all in perfect detail. His powers of observation were keen, and his words painted an amazingly accurate picture of Rome, much to Yovanix's delight.

I sat down next to them, content to listen to Paul's bright chatter. My belly was getting bigger, and I wondered if I were carrying twins. I hoped not; twins tended to come early, and I wanted time to see Pompeii and get back to Alexandria before giving birth. I did a quick calculation in my head, and decided I had fifteen weeks before the baby arrived. A tiny kick made me grin. I loved being pregnant and feeling a new life bloom within me. It was a miracle each time it happened, no matter how common an occurrence it was. I wondered if 'common miracle' was an oxymoron, then decided not.

After sitting for a while, I felt more energetic and decided to go for a short walk along the docks. I was interested in the other wares and boats. There were nearly twenty of them docked, and more were pressing from behind. Small skiffs were rowed back and forth as customs officials, fishermen, and traders jockeyed for position at the docks. Goods arrived from all over the known world. I caught a whiff of spices and headed in that direction. There was a flash of red-gold as a brilliant scarf was unfolded, and a donkey brayed loudly, adding to the cacophony of men's and women's voices arguing and bargaining.

People stared as I walked by. I was still an oddity. Now, far from the north, I stuck out again. My platinum hair and icy eyes were drawing overt glances from everyone. However, I paid no attention. I bent over a basket of brightly coloured wool skeins, and then admired an exquisite vase made from Phoenician glass. It was striped like a zebra on top, black and white, and like a tiger on the base, yellow and black. There were other vases and lamps, but this one caught my eye, and I wished I could buy it for Alexander. He would have loved its sparkling beauty.

The trader saw my covetous gaze and he barked out a price that seemed astronomical. I shook my head, making a face. I moved on, past screaming parrots tied to a large branch, past cheap rugs woven from reeds, and some more expensive carpets made from wool, until I arrived at the end of the dock where two or three boats vied for the little space that was left. They were trying to unload in unison, everyone crying out, pushing and shoving his neighbour aside.

Suddenly a sack of beans spilled over and a flood of dried peas made footing treacherous. There came a loud splash as a merchant skidded off the dock. His armload of feather dusters shot into the air like a flock of ungainly egrets. I backed out of the way as another person stepped on the peas and slithered wildly. He hadn't been carrying anything, but to save himself from falling, he grabbed a man holding two bales of cotton, and they both went down with a resounding thud. The bales of cotton bounced, hitting another man in the back, and he in turn fell into the arms of a stout matron who had been shopping on the docks. She dropped her basket of goods, and eggs broke and apples rolled as she shrieked. Another fellow dived for the apples and crashed into a large cage that popped open with a splintering sound. Out bounded three large baboons, obviously thrilled to get free, and even more excited by the noise and fuss. Utter pandemonium broke out as the apes leapt into the crowd, tails held high and wicked teeth bared in huge grins. I turned and ran, not wishing to become entangled in the fracas. People were coming from everywhere, trying to catch a glimpse of the action or trying to see what was going on.

I had to fight through a growing crowd of bystanders. I was torn between wanting to laugh aloud and real fright; I was six months pregnant and didn't fancy a tumble or a fall into the water. I could swim; but there were boats everywhere and I didn't want to get run into.

Suddenly a strong arm reached out and grabbed me, pulling me through the crowd. 'Down here!' came a voice I didn't recognize, and I was half shoved, half carried off the dock and onto a low barge.

My first reaction was to scream, but then I realized I was free of the crowd and the narrow dock. I turned to thank my saviour and saw it was the merchant with the striped glass. He bowed very low and his tall, pointed cap nearly fell off his head.

'It was getting terribly crowded on the dock,' he said, 'and I had to move my precious merchandise. I saw you, and decided you looked precious too. Like one of my finer vases. Did you see this one?' He lifted the corner of a linen sheet and uncovered a scintillating blue vase made of transparent glass in all the hues of tropical, turquoise water. I uttered a gasp.

'That is very lovely,' I admitted, ducking as an apple came flying through the air. 'Maybe you'd better store the glass down below until things calm down.'

'I think I'd better.' The merchant clapped his hands and a slave poked his head out of the hatch. 'Start putting the fragile goods back in the crates. We'll skip the dock market for now; we'll set up again when things calm down, and if they don't, we'll take some glass to the salt market this evening.' The slave began to pack everything up and I helped. After all, the merchant had saved me – I could help save a few cups and plates.

The uproar on the docks had not abated. Policemen were now trying to calm everyone, and people were falling off the docks into the water with loud splashes.

'I hope my husband is not too worried about me,' I said, trying to catch a glimpse of Alexander. I could make out the prow of the dragon ship rising high into the air, but I couldn't see anyone I knew in the crowd.

'Come below deck. Just sit here for a moment, you'll be safer. Yousaff! Get the lady a cool drink! You look pale, are you feeling all right?'

I nodded and sat on a low stool covered with a beautiful tapestry. The slave Yousaff poured me a drink from a glass pitcher that had been standing in a brass bucket filled with water. I took it and drank gratefully; it was fresh orange juice with a touch of spice mixed in it. 'Thank you, I was thirsty,' I admitted.

'Have you been shopping all morning? Where are your goods? Did you lose them in the bustle? Shall I send Yousaff to fetch them?'

'No, I had nothing with me. However, if you would be so kind to give a message to the captain of the dragon boat, Phaleria, and tell her I'm here. I don't want anyone to worry about me.'

'Excellent idea. I will go myself. A loud smash sounded from the docks as an amphora hit the wood and shattered. The trader winced, bowed low, and said, 'I forgot to introduce myself. David, glass and papyrus trader from Byblos.'

'I hope that it wasn't your amphora that just broke,' I said.

'No, I don't believe it was. Yousaff, guard the lady. I'll be back shortly. Would you like a litter or some guards to accompany you to your boat?'

'No, honestly, I feel so silly. I'll just walk back myself when calm is restored. I would go now, but I'm pregnant, and I don't think it would be a good idea to get pushed into the harbour.'

'The gods blessed you! How wonderful. I congratulate your family.' He beamed and made a sign with his hand, another god-sign that I'd never seen. I didn't ask him what it was. It was considered rude to notice those quick motions made when the gods must be either appeased or thanked. I sipped my orange juice and relaxed, letting my gaze wander around the inside of the richly furnished boat. It was full of many beautiful glass objects: bottles; cups; perfume flasks; vases; and lamps. One lamp swung from a short chain attached to the ceiling with a little pulley, so it could be raised or lowered over the low square table in the centre of the room. The table was carved from massive wood and inlaid with ivory and coral around the edges. Precious writing materials were arranged in gilded boxes, and sheets of papyrus were carefully stacked next to them. On the floor sat four large pillows, one on each side of the table. They were covered with tapestry and embroidered with bright wool. On my right there was a bed covered with rugs and furs. Beneath it was a large wooden drawer where the glassware had been stored, and baskets woven from dark brown reeds lined the walls. There were wooden boxes carefully marked to show their contents, and a snowfall of pale woodchips on the floor attested to the fact that the fragile glass was often packed in sawdust.

Alexander had told me that the best papyrus came from Byblos, and that the Greeks called it biblos, the root of words like 'bibliotheca' and 'bible', which meant library and book. The Romans would take those words for their own, and in my time, in France for example; you went to a bibliothèque to borrow books. Parchment, vellum, and then paper would gradually replace the scrolls of papyrus, but right now the best place to buy writing materials was Byblos.

The glass was amazing too. I admired the goblet I was holding. Before the Phoenicians came along and started making glass, it had been opaque. The Phoenicians had a high percentage of quartz in their sand and the glass they made was transparent. They added different elements to make brilliant colours and were the most talented glassmakers in the world. They moulded it, spun it, cut and polished it, and made exquisite objects. Fragile, and nearly all lost to time. I contemplated a shipment of glass that would have cost a fortune in my own era. Museums would have fought wars to get the pitcher made of scintillating pink quartz glass beaded with sparkles of palest green, blue, and yellow glass along the sides. The handle was braided, made of perfectly clear glass, and the spout was carefully formed to catch the last drop.

It was a heavy object. Yousaff carried it with his two hands, and he was reverently careful when he picked it up and put it down.

I finished my juice and gave the cup back to Yousaff, who took it with a little bow. I thanked him and he nodded. 'Would you like more?' he asked, in cultured Greek.

My face must have reflected my surprise, because he smiled wryly. 'I was not always a slave,' he said. 'My parents were rich merchants in Tyre.'

'How did you become a slave then?' I asked.

'When Alexander the Conqueror vanquished the city, my tribe was massacred and I was sold into slavery. I was still a child then, only thirteen years old.'

'Alexander did that? Oh, how dreadful.' My voice cracked.

I swore I would live to avenge my family, but fate decided otherwise. The perfidious king died nearly two years ago in Babylon, long may his shade suffer. I heard say that they forgot to put gold in his mouth, and that his funeral cortège was stolen by Ptolemy, then disappeared.

He never had a funeral. I suppose I should feel satisfied, but I don't. I feel cheated.'

I swallowed with an effort. 'But, didn't you take refuge in the temples?'

'We could not; we were not Phoenicians but Greek, and their temples were closed to us. The only Greek temple was full. We fought alongside the soldiers of the city. But we were defeated, and the people who had not taken refuge in the temples were sold into slavery or executed.'

'How dreadful,' I whispered. 'What about the rest of your family?'

'I don't know what happened to them. I was stunned by a rock,' he pointed to a scar on his temple, 'and when I woke up I was on a ship being taken to the coast where I was sold to a merchant. He took me to Byblos and there the glass merchant bought me. I never had the chance to find out what happened to my family.'

'But is there a chance they are still in Tyre? Did you ever write to ask?'

He looked at me and frowned. 'I have no idea to whom I could write. They could be slaves, and in that case, they will have new names. On the other hand, they could all be dead. I really have no idea what happened to them. Someday I will go back to Tyre and find out. Until then, I bide my time. My future is not to remain a slave. Soon I will be able to buy my freedom.'

'What will you do then?' I asked, torn between pity and horror.

'What I really wish is a chance for revenge. In my tribe, revenge was the most sacred duty. He is dead, but I will curse Alexander and his family until the day I die.' His voice was little more than a hiss at the end of his speech. At that moment, David called for him to go on an errand. Yousaff gave a little bow and left quickly.

I closed my eyes and leaned back against the cushions. I felt ill. The sweet juice left me nauseated, and the rocking of the boat didn't help. Suddenly, I wanted to get off, to find Alexander, to have his strong arms around me, and hear him tell me that everything was going to be fine. Perhaps it was because I'd half started believing in gods and fate. A curse was not something to be taken lightly. My children and I were part of Alexander's family, and therefore on the receiving end of the slave's curse.

My heartbeat returned to normal, my stomach settled. I took a shaky breath and decided it was simply shock making me feel so nervous. I was glad when I heard Alexander's and David's voices and footsteps on the deck. I glanced at the doorway. Alexander ducked through, his face tense. When he saw me he relaxed and I saw his shoulders slump.

'Ashley, I was so worried.'

'I was caught in the crowd and David let me rest here.'

'He told me about it. It was very kind of him. You look pale, are you feeling well?' He took my hand and sat next to me. I leaned my head on his shoulder and sighed contentedly.

'I'm all right now. I wasn't too alarmed, not for myself at least, but I was anxious for the baby.' I patted my tummy. 'Shall we go back to the boat? I feel a need to rest.'

'There's no room in the boat. Phaleria has turned it into a boutique and her wares are unpacked. We shall have to go back to the Roman's villa.' He saw my look of dismay and kissed me. 'Don't worry; I will order a litter.'

'Alex, we don't have any money,' I said in a whisper. Litters were terribly expensive. Four people carried them, and they were used by the very wealthy to get around in. Decrepit old women favoured them. So did courtesans. 'Don't bother about a litter. I can ride back in the chariot with Polliana.'

'He's gone back to the villa.'

'Then I'll walk. We can just go slowly.'

'No, I won't have you losing your babe. Remember what happened in Ecbatana? You must rest now. I'll go find a litter and you relax. Do you want me to send you Plexis and Paul? They are helping Phaleria, but I'm sure she can spare them.'

I did remember Ecbatana, and the miscarriage that I suffered there. I had lost a baby because I'd been walking and riding too much. The memory was a painful one. I'd been so happy to have a child; Paul had been in the clutches of Darius, and I'd thought we'd never find him. Unfortunately, I'd miscarried, and my next child, a little girl, had died when she was just three months old. Now I had three children: Paul, whom we'd finally found in Nysa; Chiron, my bright-eyed boy; and Cleopatra, my little ice-maiden. A fourth baby was on the way. It was my sixth pregnancy which was a normal number of pregnancies for this era, given my age and health. Children didn't die as easily as they would in the Middle Ages. Medicine was actually more effective; the Greeks and Arabs had many remedies. Unfortunately, science would vanish, not to be discovered again until modern times. The Middle Ages, aptly termed the Dark Ages, were years of ignorance and fear. A little ice age would make the climate a terrible hardship, and religion would make science a sin. Luckily, I was in an age of enlightenment. I patted Alexander's arm.

'I'll be fine by myself. Are you sure you can pay for a litter?' I frowned at him.

He shrugged. 'I'll think of something. Until then, stay here. I'll send Plexis for you.'

I peered through the doorway. The deck was empty. Had the slave seen him? I wondered, worried for some reason.

He kissed me tenderly and then left. For a minute, he stood in the doorway looking back at me, his face in the darkness of the hold. Then he disappeared into the bright sunlight. The last I saw of him was his shadow, slipping silently up the stairs.

I don't know why I felt such tightness in my chest, as if he were going into danger. Whatever the reason, I wouldn't be comforted. When the glass merchant came back, thankfully with Plexis in tow, I was nearly frantic with worry.

'It's nothing, just my nerves,' I explained, hastily wiping my face with my hem.

The slave Yousaff looked at me queerly. Had he caught a glimpse of the man who'd conquered Tyre and destroyed his world? I hoped not. I felt completely disoriented, as if the day were a dream. I put my hand on my forehead, but no, I had no fever. Perhaps it was simply my hormones getting the better of me. In any case, I hoped it would soon pass. I stood shakily and bade the glass merchant and his slave 'goodbye'. Plexis helped me up the stairs and held my elbow as we walked back towards the boat. Once there he made me a seat in the shade and gave me a fan made of brightly dyed egret feathers.

'Where did you get that?' I asked.

'Paul found it floating in the water near the stern of the boat. Are you feeling better? We were anxious about you. I wish you wouldn't wander around alone. Please tell me next time, I'll accompany you.' His handsome face was serious. For once, his eyes had lost their teasing sparkle.

I nodded. 'I'm sorry, I wasn't thinking. Where has Alexander gone?'

'To fetch a litter.'

'How will he pay for it?'

'I haven't the faintest idea,' he said with a shrug, 'but don't worry, he'll think of something.'

I told him about the slave and his face grew dark.

'Do you think he recognized him?'

'I don't see how. Remember, he is officially dead. Even Ptolemy hardly recognized him when he went to the palace. The slave will simply think it's someone who looks like him. Tyre was taken when Iskander was still young. He's changed since then. His hair is much darker and he has a different walk, thanks to his shattered ankle.'

'That's true,' I said reflectively. 'He has changed. Moreover, he's changed since Babylon. He's so much calmer now, so … so,' I searched for a word.

'Reasonable?' Plexis asked, wrinkling his nose. 'Is that the word you were looking for?'

I grinned wryly. 'I would like to ask Demos how he recognized Alexander after twelve years. It was a complete surprise.'

'Demos identified him because he knew him well. A man fighting in the heat of a battle would not.'

'There is something about that slave though; he's different from anyone I've met in this time. He gives me the impression of … oh, you're going to think I'm foolish, but he's like someone from my own time. He's angry. He doesn't feel as if he deserves to be a slave.'

'That's normal, no one feels as if they *deserve* to be a slave.' Plexis didn't sound concerned.

'Yes, but they accept their fate, this man does not.'

'You sound so sure of yourself. How long did you speak to him? A few minutes? You must have misunderstood.'

'No, I know what I'm saying.' I stared moodily into the water. I felt tense and wished I knew why.

The shadows grew long. Alexander didn't reappear, and even Plexis cast apprehensive glances at the crowd milling on the docks. Paul brought me a piece of flatbread wrapped around strips of spicy fish. We had cool water to drink and a slice of watermelon for dessert. Plexis stayed with me until the sun had nearly set, then he decided to go into the city to search for his friend. However, we had no idea what had happened to Alexander and no idea where to look for him.

Phaleria would trade until it grew too dark, then she would be occupied putting everything away again. Her crew was busy as well, even with Paul and Yovanix helping as best they could. Yovanix was blind, but knew where everything went, and had memorized each corner of the dragon boat. He manoeuvred about with such ease that when I saw him I was hard put to remember he had no sight.

Demos saw Plexis leave and came to reassure me. He was a big bear of a man, but kind-hearted. Seeing my unease he put aside his chore and sat next to me for a while. He told me not to fret, but everyone had been saying the same thing to me since Alexander had left. I was still worried. Where was Alexander? Why hadn't he returned? And where was the glass-merchant? It didn't make sense. He should have put his wares back out on the dock, but now that the crowd had thinned I could see that there was nothing in front of his boat, and the boat itself looked deserted.

'Demos, I'm going to go see if the glass-merchant is still there.' I pointed towards the Phoenician's ship.

Demos raised his eyebrows, so I explained what had happened when I'd met the slave. Now he looked startled. 'I saw that man heading into the city right after Iskander,' he said. 'And the merchant left soon afterwards.'

'They haven't come back?'

'No, I didn't see them.'

'Were they carrying their wares?' I asked. I had overheard them talking about the salt market, so maybe they had gone there.

'Yes, they were both carrying large bundles.'

I didn't question his statement. He was naturally observant, and if he saw them leave then I believed him. I was still apprehensive though. 'Tell me, Demos, when you saw Iskander for the first time in twelve years, did you have any doubts who he was?'

'No, it was a shock, to be sure, but I had no doubts. Once you've seen Iskander you can never forget him. He has a glow that ordinary men do not have. He shines like the sun, and he holds his head a certain way. Even from afar, I recognized him in battle. And there, at the inn, I saw right away it was him.'

'That's what I was afraid of,' I said looking towards the city where the bells in the temple of Jupiter, Juno, and Minerva had started to ring. The sun was setting and the tiled rooftops were blood-red.

'I'll finish here, and then I'll go to Rome. Perhaps I'll discover something.'

'Plexis left nearly two hours ago,' I said, looking at the long shadows. I shivered. 'I have a terrible feeling about this.'

Phaleria and Demos packed up their goods, then Demos went with Vix, Titte, and Kell into the city. Erati and Oppi slung wicker baskets over their arms and went to buy food and said they'd check the salt market to see if the glass merchant was there.

An hour dragged by. Paul sat by my side, alternately telling me not to worry, and fretting about his father.

131

Everyone came back with no news at all. They had looked in the taverns, they had asked everyone they'd met, and they'd even gone into the public baths.

'I went to the salt market and saw no sign of the Phoenician,' said Oppi regretfully. 'But he may have sold all his goods and gone to an inn for the evening, or to one of the temples to pray.'

I thanked him for looking, and he waved away my words with his massive hands, then asked Paul if he wanted to go fishing with him. Paul cast a quick glance in my direction then nodded.

He and Oppi made a strange pair as they set off to fish. Paul looked civilized, and Oppi was a hairy, red-bearded barbarian with tattoos on his hands and arms. He also wore a heavy torque around his neck, had slung a sheepskin over his shoulders in guise of a shirt, and wore a leather kilt. They both carried fishing poles and bait, and Paul was laughing at something Oppi said.

Phaleria asked Erati to cook dinner, and the others relaxed after their busy day. Phaleria sat next to me and took my hand. 'Don't worry, I'm sure he's all right. He's fought battles against great odds, crossed the mountains at the end of the earth in wintertime, and survived the terrible Gedrosian desert. There's nothing like that here!'

I looked at her and tried to smile. 'I know, it does seem silly doesn't it? He's gone through so much. What could possibly happen to him here?' Two tears trickled down my cheeks. 'I'm afraid,' I admitted. 'The closer we get to Alexandria, the more frightened I become. He has gone so far and done so much. He's lost so much. His empire, his family, his soul ...'

'We got that back,' Phaleria reminded me seriously.

I bit my lip. 'In my dreams he's wearing a blindfold and there's a strange clown standing near him.'

'I don't understand,' she said.

'Neither do I,' I admitted slowly, 'but I never understood dreams.'

'What's a "clown"?'

'A clown is a person dressed in bright colours who makes you laugh. Sometimes they're funny and sometimes they're sad. I was always afraid of them,' I said, shaking my head. 'I wish I knew why I dream about a harlequin clown with Iskander.'

'Perhaps you should ask Vix,' she told me, nodding her head towards the man dressed in pale grey robes standing by the bow. He was looking up, and his sharp profile seemed etched on the darkening sky. He had long black hair, braided in a single plait that reached his waist. He shaved his beard but wore a long moustache that gave him a mournful air. He was probably looking for a sign in the sky or water that would lead us to Alexander.

Vix was a Gaul, trained as a druid, and always interpreting the signs around him. A simple bird could mean something depending on what it was doing or what sort it was, and dreams were carefully discussed. For Vix, dreams were messages from worlds that we could only get glimpses of through drug-induced trances or sleep.

I was doubtful. Even after twelve years in a world where the supernatural was matter-of-course, I still had trouble

133

believing in dreams and oracles. Part of my mind wanted to believe, but I had been born and educated in a land ruled by machines and science. Apollo didn't have a chance, no matter how many times he spoke to me. I would always believe that the swirling smoke in the tiny rooms was a hallucinogen. I dreamt every night, but that didn't make the world I entered when I slept any more real, and the supernatural would always be a dream-state for me, a figment of my imagination.

I held up my hand and stared at it. One of my hands was missing at the wrist; an ivory hand was fastened onto my forearm with leather straps. It was beautifully carved and graceful. The ivory was the same fair colour as my skin, and even the nails had been carefully shaped and tinted with rose. You had to look at it carefully to perceive that it was in fact a fake hand, an illusion. I clenched my fist, but the ivory hand didn't move. It was a chimera, as were my dreams.

Oppi and Paul didn't take very long to catch dinner. As soon as they each landed two fish, they cleaned and filleted their catch and brought them back for Erati to cook. Oppi tousled Paul's hair and patted his back, nearly sending him reeling off the boat. 'A good fisherman, he is!' he bellowed fondly.

Paul grinned, winced, and went to the back of the boat to clean his tackle. Then he looked up and gave a shout from his post at the stern. 'It's Plexis! He's come back!' I leapt to my feet, my heart pounding.

Plexis didn't waste words. 'I didn't find him.' His voice was bleak. 'I'm sorry. I sent a message to the Roman's villa, and I'll go there as soon as I eat something. You stay here on the boat.'

I was shaking so badly I couldn't answer for a moment. 'Where could he be?' I finally managed to whisper. No one answered. We were silent while we ate, even Demos. He sat like a taciturn mountain on the deck, his broad shoulders seeming capable of supporting the weight of the world. I wished he could lessen the weight of my disquiet. Plexis finished his bowl of fish stew and stood, wiping his mouth with his napkin. 'I'll be back before midnight,' he promised, stroking my hair. 'Don't fuss any more, try and rest.' He turned towards Phaleria. 'Will you stay on board tonight or will you go to the inn?'

'We'll stay here. I'll send Titte and Kell to the inn, they might hear something there.'

Plexis hesitated, then bent down and kissed my mouth. 'We'll find him,' he said, 'Iskander didn't disappear into thin air.' His eyes were kind.

'Aren't you afraid something has happened to him?' I questioned.

'What could possibly happen to a battle-scarred soldier in such a civilized city?' he asked, trying to lift my spirits.

Suddenly a loud voice soared above the babble. A newscaster trotted up to the docks on a skinny piebald pony, a roll of parchment held at arm's length in front of his face. Slaves stood in front of him and beat drums, punctuating his words. He was calling out the latest news. A clamour rose into the air, as people heard what the man was crying out. My skin suddenly prickled.

'Did he just say what I think he did?' I whispered. Plexis stood up slowly. On board our boat, the people who understood Latin suddenly leapt to their feet while the others tugged on sleeves and begged to know what was happening.

'It's not true,' I said brokenly, 'Oh, Plexis, tell me it's not what I think.'

'It's an announcement from the Circus Maximus,' he whispered. 'By Hermes and Aries, what a terrible trick to play. They're saying Iskander has returned from Hades, that he has been captured, and that he will fight tomorrow night in a special show.'

'Is he serious? Does he believe that Alexander has come back from the dead?' I felt as if my bones were turning to ice.

'No, It's a publicity stunt to sell tickets. However, we know it's the truth, even if the public doesn't. Iskander was captured though, that much is true. Now we know what happened to him.'

We stared at each other. 'The slave,' I said, 'it was the slave. He did recognize him and he's taken his revenge. Quickly, Plexis, we don't have much time. Go to Augustus, tell him it's a mistake, or tell him it's the truth; and that if Iskander does die, Ptolemy will raze Rome. Oh, I don't know what to do!' I moaned.

'Tell Demos to go to get the *lanista*,' said Plexis cryptically.

'The who?'

Plexis told me, then left. I called my son over and took his chin firmly in my hand. 'We must keep our heads if we

136

mean to help your father,' I said. 'I want you and Demos to go into the city and try to find the man who organizes the games. There must be someone in charge, and he shouldn't be too hard to find. Could you go to fetch him?'

'The *lanista*? Yes, I think that he might help us.' Demos told me.

'What's a *lanista*?' Paul asked.

'The superintendent of the gladiators.' Demos said pensively. 'I'll not lie to you, My Lady. If Iskander is slated to fight tomorrow, there is not much we can do to stop it.'

A few minutes later, a slender boy and a mountain of a man walked off through the gathering darkness. I watched them leave with my mouth twisted awry. The problem was ignorance. I had no idea how the Romans organized their games, how the actors were chosen, and what happened in the arena. Stories of lions, gladiators, and armed combatants sprang to mind. I started pacing, then sat down next to Phaleria and leaned against her warm shoulder.

'Do you think he has a chance to win his fight?' I asked.

'It depends on whom he's fighting,' she said reasonably.

'I'd like to get my hands on that slave,' I said darkly.

'Demos has already sent Oppi to search for him.'

I raised my eyebrows. I hadn't noticed that Oppi had left the boat. 'When?'

'Right after Plexis left. I think Demos wants a little chat with that slave.'

'I suppose he thought that he was just doing his sacred duty,' I said glumly.

'Do you want to talk to Vix now?' she asked.

I scratched my head. 'Do you think it will help?'

'He sees things others do not, even if you don't truly believe. It can't hurt to listen. Besides, he knows the customs of the Circus Maximus. He can tell you about them at least.'

Vix was speaking to Yovanix. I didn't want to interrupt, but he motioned me to his side. 'I was just going to tell Yovanix about the circus,' he said. 'If you want to know more, sit here and listen.'

I didn't argue. Vix was a druid, which meant he was a teacher as well as a priest. In Gallic *oppida* – fortified settlements – the druids were the only ones who could read and write, letters being sacred things used to cast spells.

Vix reached into his pouch and took out a handful of dried herbs. He crushed them in his hands, releasing their sharp scent, and then tossed them to the four cardinal points, reciting a short prayer to the gods of stories and history. I asked him what herbs he used, and he let me smell them and try to guess. Mostly it was rosemary, used throughout the centuries for remembrance.

'The story I will tell you has its roots in Greece,' he began. 'Before the opening of the funeral games in honour of his friend Patroclus, Achilles immolated on the funeral pyre four noble mares, two of his favourite hounds, and twelve sons of the Trojans. This version of Patroclus's funeral would forever haunt the Etruscans.'

'Wait a minute,' I interrupted, 'what do the Etruscans have to do with this? We're in Rome, aren't we?'

Vix peered at me, his grey eyes sharp. He didn't mind my interruptions; he was used to my incessant questions. 'The Etruscans were here long before the Romans. They were the ones who built the Circus Maximus, three hundred years ago. They believe that the dead live in a world contiguous with the one we live in. The dead are highly honoured in Etruscan society, and for them the funeral is almost like a rebirth. To send their loved ones off in the best possible style is one of their major preoccupations. That and music.'

'Music?'

'I'm getting to that. Where was I? Oh yes, Patroclus's funeral. The Etruscans sought to enhance their mourning by raising it to the level of the Greek legend, and they consoled themselves for the mortal condition of humanity through the enchantments of music and poetry. And a furious lust for blood. The Etruscans used to sacrifice prisoners on the funeral pyres of their dead, but then they started to have them fight in front of the pyres, giving the prisoners a chance to live.

'The current games come from an ancient and mysterious ritual. They are a manifestation of something called "The Game of Phersu.".'

'Phersu?' Now Yovanix interrupted. He turned his blind face towards me and frowned. 'I've heard of a *phersu*, it is a mask.'

'"Phersu" means mask, yes, but it also stands for the man who *wears* the mask.'

A cold breeze tickled the back of my neck. 'What man wears a mask during the games?' I asked.

'The Phersu. The word comes from further back in time than we can imagine. In the beginning there was the Mask, an infernal demon whose name is connected with that of

Persephone, the terrible Queen of Ice and Darkness. He is the most ancient of the devils, the same devils that decorate the tombs of the Etruscans. Charon, Orcus, Tulchulcha are a few of their names, and they are present in the parade opening the games. However, Phersu is their leader and their chief. During the games he stands near the blind man and watches him die.'

I was startled. 'The blind man? Is he really blind, or does he wear a blindfold?' I asked, my heart beating fast.

'He wears a blindfold. Why?'

'In my dream I saw Iskander standing in the middle of a great clearing. He was wearing a dark sack over his head, and just behind him stood a harlequin clown. The clown stood still, simply looking on. He gave me the chills.'

'What did he look like?' Vix's voice was tense; he leaned forward, taking my shoulders in his hands. 'How was this clown you speak of dressed?'

'He wore a short jacket, checked with alternate light and dark patches. His pants were ragged. He had a pointed hat with a little pompom on the top. And his mask was a black domino, just covering the top of his face.' I faltered, 'It was – it looked exactly like the harlequin clowns of my time. He couldn't have voyaged intact through the ages, could he have?'

Vix's hands tightened on my shoulders. Then he released them and leaned back. 'Phersu is a very powerful demon. You have just described his costume perfectly, although sometimes he wears a Phrygian helmet, and sometimes he wears a silken beard tied onto his mask. He presides over the games and looks on without pity or emotion as the men die. He represents the horror of death, which must be vanquished by mirth, the fat demon, who will come after the massacre to chase away Phersu.'

'What will happen tomorrow?' I asked.

'The ceremony starts with a parade. Then there are the games, they last until all the prisoners have fought. Then there is the closing ceremony when Phersu is chased out of the arena.

'However, to know exactly what will happen we must find out if they are funeral games, in honour of an Etruscan citizen, or if they are the Roman games, which are mostly horse racing and fighting between professional gladiators. The Etruscans, I warn you, are a strange people. Their rituals are intimately linked with death and dying, yet at the same time they celebrate life with an almost constant outpouring of music. They play their flutes to everything, from kneading their bread to beating their slaves; everything has a set rhythm and melody. The music must be followed exactly, to vary it would destroy the delicate harmonic balance between life and death.'

'So you're saying that if the ceremony tomorrow is Etruscan, we will have no chance to change it?'

'That's what I'm saying, yes. They will do everything to appease the Phersu. Nothing must change.'

'The Mask,' said Yovanix, shuddering. 'He sounds terrible.'

'He is,' said Vix, seriously.

The night was full of light and laughter. People walked around the docks carrying small, portable lanterns or torches. In the city, I could see slaves lighting the streetlights with long tapers. From the boat next to ours came the strains of a flute and songs accompanying a banquet.

Then came the sound of hooves clattering on stone. Someone was coming in a great hurry. It was Plexis; he slid off his lathered pony and tossed its reins to Titte, who'd jumped onto the dock to greet him. Clattering behind him came Augustus, who dismounted as well. The Roman was wrapped in an impressive purple cape and wearing his official helmet. I felt a glimmer of hope. His garb meant that he was here on authoritative business.

'Has Demos returned yet?' Plexis asked me, as he clambered aboard.

'Not yet,' I said. 'Can Augustus help us?'

'He's not sure. He has to speak to the *lanista*.' Plexis waved to Titte, who was still holding the horses. 'Can you find water for them?' To me, he said, 'When did Demos leave?'

'Right after you did, nearly two hours ago.'

Augustus came over and patted my shoulder. 'We rode as fast as we could.'

'Thank you. How are Scipio and Hirkan?' I asked.

'Fine, just fine. They wanted to come with us, but I told them they had to wait behind. Scipio has now sworn to save Iskander …' he faltered and lowered his voice. 'Plexis told me that it really is Iskander, the great conqueror, back from the dead. Is it *de facto*? How can it be true? Did you know that some of the gladiators swear that they were soldiers in his army? Perhaps he will meet someone he knows in the arena.'

I gaped at him. Finally I said, 'Iskander has changed. He's not the same man who conquered Persia and went to India. When his death was announced, he was so ill that he was actually dying. We managed to save his life, but the gods banished him from his kingdom for all time. You mustn't breathe a word of this to anyone, ever. Not even to your wife.' I figured that I would put the blame on the gods. Otherwise, Augustus would certainly think that Alexander was a coward for running away from his duty as king. However, Augustus lived in a republic. The Romans didn't believe in kings and absolute monarchs any more than the Greeks did. They did however, believe in the gods.

Augustus scratched his chin thoughtfully. 'If the public finds out that it is truly Iskander in the arena, they will not let him leave it alive. They will have him fight against impossible odds. I should think that would be a thrilling combat, if it weren't your husband,' he added apologetically.

'You seem to take this very calmly,' I told him, folding my arms across my chest and trying to keep the acid out of my voice. A thrilling combat indeed, as if Alexander hadn't fought enough in his life.

He gave an expressive shrug. 'We heard many stories about King Iskander; one of them said he hadn't died. A certain oracle insisted he had gone north to the lands of the Eaters of the Dead. Then the seer died, and the stories died with her. It was a very important oracle; she saw the future in bolts of lightning. Other stories praised his valour and strength. Most of the people won't believe it's really he though, you see, already at least ten other Iskanders have fought in the Circus Maximus since he died. It's a ploy to attract spectators, nothing else, but the people expect a good actor and a good show.'

'What happened to the other Iskanders?' I asked.

'They died. Not one survived the Game of Phersu.'

I closed my eyes. I'd heard all I wanted about the Game of Phersu, presided by the Mask, the horrifying minion of Persephone. 'Well, if he's my minion perhaps I can meet him and speak to him,' I said with a shiver.

'No one can meet him. No one knows who he is, even the *lanista*. Most think he's a supernatural being who appears for the games and returns to the Underworld when they are finished.'

'Oh really?' My voice dripped ice. I felt my temper slipping. Luckily, Plexis took my elbow and drew me away with a murmured excuse to Augustus.

'Ashley, he's only trying to help. When the *lanista* gets here, Augustus will ask to have the game officially annulled.'

'Do you think he will succeed?'

'Do you want the truth?' he asked gently, his eyes sad. I nodded mutely and he said, 'no, I don't think he will succeed. The games are too important.'

I stared at him, then turned and went down into the hold. I didn't want to hear the *lanista* telling Augustus that the games would go on as planned. I didn't want to hear the words that would condemn my husband to die, blindfolded and alone, in the middle of an arena.

Vix gave me a sleeping draught. I don't know if it was the wisest thing I could do, but my eyes were burning and my head felt as if it were filled with ashes. I knew I would lie awake and fret, so I drank the bitter potion and curled up on a soft blanket. The slight rocking of the boat and the drink put me to sleep.

I dreamed. I dreamt I was standing in the middle of a sandy circle. Around me was darkness, but I heard the cheers and shouts of a huge crowd. I stood still. In my hand was a leash, and on the end of the leash was a huge dog, bigger than any dog I'd ever seen. It looked like a cross between a wolfhound and a mastiff. It turned its head and looked at me with glowing red eyes, drawing its lips back in a silent snarl. Sharp, white teeth were bared. The hair on its back rose in a prickly crest, and I saw its whole body vibrating as it suddenly collected itself and sprang into the air. I held onto the leash, stunned, as I saw whom the beast had attacked. Alexander stood in front of me, his hands fastened behind his back, a black hood covering his face, blind and helpless before the savage attack.

I pulled back on the leash, meaning to stop the dog, but the leash somehow became tangled around Alexander's legs and hampered him even more. The dog bit huge chunks out of his flesh while he screamed and screamed.

The screams woke me up, but they were my own.

Plexis was shaking me, begging me to be quiet.

I sat up and drew a shaking hand across my sweaty brow. 'I'm sorry,' I gasped, leaning my head against his chest. 'Did I wake everyone up? What time is it?'

'It's nearly dawn. No one was sleeping anyway; we've been talking, trying to figure out what to do.'

'Augustus couldn't stop the games.' It was a statement, not a question. Plexis nodded, his chin resting on my head.

'I'm sorry,' he whispered, his arms tightening around my shoulders. 'He tried his best, but he doesn't have much power here. The games are vital.'

'So is Iskander,' I said, my voice breaking. 'I don't want him to die.'

'Neither do I.'

'Are they to be Roman games or Etruscan games?'

'Roman. At least we have that much more hope. Augustus did promise never to tell anyone that Iskander didn't die. If they do find out, they will hunt him down and kill him. The Romans are afraid of him. They think that if he had lived, he would have invaded Rome. Augustus says that rumour has it he was poisoned by a Roman spy.'

I stayed in his arms until the sun rose. The light seemed cruel to me. If only I could have held onto the night, in the darkness Alexander had a chance. In less than six hours, under the blazing noonday sun, he would enter the arena. During the night, Axiom returned from the Roman's villa. With him were Scipio and Hirkan. The two boys huddled with Paul at the stern of the dragon boat. They sat together, their heads touching, speaking in hushed voices. Next to the three boys was Yovanix. He rested a light hand on Paul's shoulder. Perilous, the puppy, lay in his lap. The sight of the hound made me shiver. My dream came back to me.

'Can we go to the Circus Maximus?' I asked Plexis. 'Is there any chance of getting tickets now?'

'Augustus took care of that last night; he used his influence to get us good seats.'

I looked at Plexis. He had deep circles under his eyes and his face was lined with fatigue. 'You must be exhausted,' I said, shaking my head. 'You searched for Iskander all evening, then you rode to the villa and back again. You've been up all night …'

'We've been keeping vigil,' he said, his smile wan.

'I'm sorry,' I said, 'I should have stayed with you. I was a coward, I preferred to sleep, I didn't want to face the hours dragging by.'

'That's good, at least you'll be able to stay awake for the games now,' he said, trying for a joke. His eyes filled with tears though, and I pulled him to me.

'Oh, Plexis, don't cry. We'll think of something, and even if we don't, I'm sure Iskander will. He's so strong; he'll dazzle us all with his victory. He'll vanquish his opponent and stand gloriously in the blinding sun while we cheer ourselves hoarse. Don't cry. Please don't cry. Lie down beside me and rest your head on my lap. I'll tickle your back for you while you rest.'

I stroked his hair, slipping my hand beneath his tunic to rub his back. After a while, his breathing evened out and he slept. I sat with his head on my lap while the sun coloured the sky progressively rose then gold. Dawn gave way to morning, as Eos, goddess of the dawn, opened the gates to the heavens, and Helios drove the chariot of the sun onto the great arc of the sky.

Axiom sat beside me, nodding silently. He too looked tired and worried, but he smiled bravely and touched my cheek. 'Don't worry,' he mouthed, 'he'll be fine.'

'I hope so,' I whispered. Then we were quiet as Rome woke up.

On the docks, the first sounds were the screeching of the gulls. They flew overhead, on their way towards the open sea, and they called to each other with shrill cries. Afterwards, the breeze picked up and the waves began to slap against the sides of the boats. Voices rose above the sound of the water as the crews awoke. Some prayed in singsong voices, welcoming the sun and the morning. Others greeted the day with gestures, filling chalices with water or wine and scattering the droplets to the four winds before offering the contents to the gods. Axiom knelt and said a heartfelt prayer to his one god, while Vix led Titte and Kell in a prayer to Lug, Celtic god of the sun. Yovanix prayed to Lug as well, and so did Phaleria. Demos prayed to Mazda, and Plexis, when he awoke, offered a cup of water to Zeus and Apollo. Paul, who had been educated by Axiom at my request, knelt and prayed next to him. I was the only godless person aboard, probably the only atheist in Rome. It only bothered me a little. I had been raised in a world that had no gods. Man had killed god, science had killed religion, and knowledge had killed the supernatural. Here though, I was free to believe what I liked. Everyone's beliefs were respected, even my unbelieving.

Chapter Nine

Plexis woke up, rubbing his hands over his face and wincing. His whiskers were prickly. He didn't usually go so long without shaving. He gave me a quick, hard kiss, then went to the back of the boat where a tub was hidden behind a curtain. I drew my knees up to my chest and hugged them. The air was getting hotter. Voices rose from all sides now, I heard the salt merchants singing as they marched to the salt flats. I stood up. I would go to the public baths; I needed to wash and wanted to change my clothes. When I went to the Circus Maximus, I wanted to look my best.

Phaleria went with me. We took our finest robes from the cedar chest in the hold. I told Paul to look for his blue tunic and silver circlet. Plexis escorted us through the crowded streets. I never would have been able to find my way. I felt light, insubstantial. My hand and feet were icy cold. We walked, yet I hardly noticed where we went.

The baths were lovely, but I can hardly remember them. I recall a large room with a tiled floor, then there was a swimming pool filled with hot water where we bathed. The Roman baths covered several blocks, with pools full of cold, warm, and hot water. There were gymnasiums, massage rooms, dressing rooms, exercise rooms, saunas, and gardens.

When I was in Rome, the baths were halfway finished. Three pools were built, as were the saunas and the exercise room. There was a changing room for women, and we were given towels made of soft linen to wrap around ourselves as we walked around the extensive grounds. Augustus had guest passes for us to use in the baths, otherwise, since we weren't Roman citizens, we wouldn't have been able to go. The baths were impressive, and to get to them, we had to walk through the Forum. When I was there, the forum contained just five temples, the senate building, and an open-air amphitheatre. There was also a stream running through it that would be diverted to create the future sewer system. In another hundred years or so, the Forum would be completed. It was already beautiful, and although I had no wish to sightsee, I couldn't help the amazed prick of interest as I passed the magnificent temples. The Romans were proficient with cement, and some of the buildings were incredibly complex. They also loved grandeur, and raised their roofs to seemingly impossible heights.

We bathed, and a slave braided my hair for me. Now and then, I would recall the dream I had about the huge dog and Alexander, and a tremor would shake my body. I couldn't eat anything; my stomach would have just given it back again. After we finished dressing, we walked slowly back to the boat. Phaleria tried to cheer me up by pointing out the sights, but I was miserable company. Finally she just put her arm around my waist, and we finished the stroll in silence. Programmes had been posted throughout the city. On the programme was the parade, fighting with professional gladiators, and the Game of Phersu, as Augustus had expected.

Once back at the boat, I sat at the bow waiting for the trumpets to blow, calling us, one and all, to the Circus Maximus and to the great games.

The Circus Maximus was an amazing place and, if I hadn't been so upset, I would have admired its architecture. It was built just beneath a hill, using the slope to its advantage, and the best seats were carved into the hill on the narrow end. Beneath the hill, large arches had been cut into the bedrock, leading to the underground passages that in turn led to the rooms where the gladiators stayed before the games. There were also pens for wild animals, and corridors large enough to drive the chariots through, two or three abreast.

Above the Circus, on the top of the hill, were temples and the beginnings of a splendid palace where, in three hundred years, the emperors of Rome would live.

I knew from my ancient history lessons, that the stadium was six hundred metres long and one hundred and ninety metres wide on the outside. Inside it was smaller, owing to the number of seats it contained. Two hundred thousand people could be crammed into the great Circus.

It was long and narrow, and the ground was sand with a long stone wall down the centre called the *spina*, around which the chariots raced. They galloped seven times around it, and the winner received a crown of laurel and a gold coin worth about ten talents.

There were twenty-four races on a normal day, but this was not a normal day. Today, Iskander, the great conqueror, was to play the Game of Phersu – although it was not a game at all. Perhaps no one believed he really was Alexander the Great. I don't think anyone truly thought he'd come back from the dead, but it made good publicity, as Demos had foreseen. The crowd was immense. The proletariat sat on wooden bleachers, while underneath, slaves packed into the section reserved for them. Nobles and dignitaries sat upon stone seats nearer the centre and close to the action. The highest notables had a special section all to themselves. We had somehow obtained seats in that sector, thanks to Augustus and his influence. Actually, he'd only managed five places. Plexis, Demos, Phaleria, and I went, and the three boys huddled together in one seat. Axiom took Yovanix to the Roman's villa, to wait for us, and Phaleria's crew stayed with the boat.

Augustus was seated near us. Elaina had made the trip from their villa, and she was perched next to him. She wore a red shawl wrapped around her head and shoulders to shield her face from the sun. She saw us and gave a wave, her expressive face reflecting our distress.

We were about fifteen feet above the sandy ground, in the second row. Our seats were carved of stone, but we rented cushions so sat comfortably enough, although my heart was pounding painfully.

We had been asked to leave any weapons at the entrance. Plexis and Demos had to give up their swords. Paul and Hirkan had reluctantly handed over their daggers, and even Phaleria had been obliged to give her ornamental knife to the man standing behind reception. Everything was carefully marked to show to whom it belonged, and we were each given receipts. We stared at them bleakly. Any hopes of leaping into the ring and defending Alexander were rapidly evaporating.

Scipio had drawn his brows in a fierce scowl and refused to acknowledge Elaina's entreaties that he sit with her. Instead he folded his arms across his chest and sat next to Paul.

Paul was wedged between Hirkan and Scipio. The three boys had become fast friends. Paul was the youngest, but as Alexander – proudly – pointed out, the tallest. Scipio had the bearing of a prince though, and his uncanny, golden eyes shot sparks at the slightest provocation. Today they were simply blazing under his glowering brows.

Hirkan was a slightly built lad, with straight, dark hair and brown eyes too big for his face. He was an easy child to like, being kind and good-humoured. He could usually lift Scipio out of his dark moods, and was wise beyond his years. Born the youngest son of a wealthy family, he'd been given to the temple at an early age to become a priest. That was common; the family would benefit from the prestige of having a priest in their ranks.

He had been happy to go to the temple and study. Quick to learn and eager to please, he'd not counted on jealousy. Hirkan was an easy-going youth, but his clever wits had made him a favourite with the low priests and the acolytes. Soon there had been rumours of training Hirkan to become a high priest. That was too much for the High Priest to accept; power was carefully hoarded in Carthage where the

High Priest had the King's ear. For a year, the priest pretended to help train Hirkan. Then the city of Carthage captured Tartessos, and a ceremony was necessary to thank the gods. The gods were fond of blood in Carthage. They were even more elated if a youth was sacrificed to them, so the Snake God was invoked and the grass mats were carefully laid upon the sand, just in front of the sacred cobra's lair.

Hirkan had been 'chosen' by the Snake God after the perfidious priest had sprinkled some oil on the boy's legs just before the ceremony. Hirkan had not thought too much about it, until the deadly cobra had glided over to him and had touched his shin with his huge, scaly head. Student priests were not supposed to be selected – normally it was a slave's child or a prisoner of war. Hirkan had not even been standing on the woven grass mat, although the High Priest had made sure the boy was nearest the cobra's den.

Hirkan had told us the story, his eyes desolate. He could never return to Carthage or face his family again. His running away was a terrible dishonour to them. He was as good as dead to his parents. It was surely very painful for him, but he tried never to let his sorrow show.

Now he turned to me and patted my knee. His kindness almost made me weep, but I managed to smile back at him. If he could be strong, so could I.

We were in the shade of the hill. The narrow end of the Circus, as I've said, was embedded in its slope. Today, since there were no races, the circus was sectioned off into two halves. A perfect circle was designed in the sand, using sticks tied with red and white ribbons. New seats were erected enclosing this circle – temporary wooden bleachers braced against the *spina*. They were in the hot sun, and most of the people sitting there held parasols over their heads. There were awnings as well, made of heavy, white cloth tied to long poles. However, these tended to block the view of those behind and disputes were always breaking out about how high they should be held. Beneath these bleachers of fortune, slaves crowded together peering through the forest of legs and feet. Many of them were gaming, throwing dice onto the sandy ground and arguing shrilly. Bets were being taken, and most people, I noted, were betting against Alexander.

I shivered. Despite the heat, I was chilled to the bone. Trumpets wailed and my skin prickled. A hush fell over the crowd and, with a clash of cymbals, the parade began.

It was strange and disquieting to see carnival costumes ushering in deadly games. I wondered if the people of those times feared death so much they had to make fun of it. They dressed their demons in bright colours, painted their faces, and laughed at their antics. But it was laughter tinged with fear, and if a clown came too close to the stands, the people would scream with fright. I saw more than one person screw his eyes shut and make the sign against evil with his hands.

Clowns have always been the link between the world of men and our nightmares. Dressed in silly clothes, a clown can lunge at another clown with a torch and set him on fire while we laugh as he bursts into flames, shrieks, and leaps towards a barrel of water. In a street, with plain clothes, the same scene would be horrifyingly macabre.

In the arena, clowns hit each other on the head with mock clubs, stabbed each other with flimsy spears, and shot harmless arrows at each other. The crowd laughed, yet the underlying emotion was fear. Shrill screams mixed in with the laughter, and nerves made some spectators, especially the women, cry.

I sat still, teeth clenched, as I watched the parade wind itself around the arena. The demons capered in and out of the grim-faced gladiators. They were walking slowly, acting as if the clowns didn't exist. For them, death was reality. The clowns only distracted from the horror. I searched for Alexander, but he was kept hidden for the grand finale. Strangely enough, the Phersu was nowhere to be seen.

There was muttering about the fact that the head demon was not in the parade. Normally, Demos told me, he led it. Silent and cold, gliding just ahead of the gladiators, looking neither left nor right, biding his time. Today he was waiting in the wings. It seemed to make the crowd even more tense. It certainly frayed my nerves.

I was wringing my hands. Well, as much as I could with one real hand and a false one made of antler. A Roman matron was sitting not far from me, and she kept glancing at our group. We did tend to stick out. Paul and I were so fair, Plexis was handsome, and today he wore a golden circlet in his chestnut hair. Demos was enormous, and Phaleria had flame-coloured tresses tied with bright ribbons.

The matron was staring at me when my false hand lost a finger. It snapped right off while I was nervously tugging on it. I held it up and looked at it dumbly. The matron's eyes rolled up in her head, and she toppled over in a faint, landing on the back of the man sitting in front of her. It caused a commotion. I was so busy watching the fuss, I missed the beginning of the games. When I turned my head back to the arena, the blessing had been completed, and a sheep was lying in a pool of blood while a priest poured barley from a golden plate onto its carcass. There was frenzied chanting and the ovine was carried to a stack of wood in the centre of the ring. Someone lit the fire, the sheep was immolated, and the gladiators took their places, two by two, around the circus.

The games would continue for as long as the pyre burned, Demos told me. I nodded. At least, I think I nodded. I couldn't feel my face, my feet, or my hand any more.

I had never watched men slaughter each other for sport. War was one thing, the gladiator games were another. At this time, the three types of people who generally became gladiators were slaves, condemned criminals, and prisoners of war. They were grim and silent. They knew that their number would probably be halved by the time the sun touched the horizon. They were fighting against men they trained with, ate with, drank with, and slept with. They knew each other. They knew their names and stories. Behind them, in the shadow cast by the hill, the clowns stood like vultures, waiting.

I had to watch. I had thought that I would shut my eyes to the horror, hide my face behind Plexis's broad shoulders, and wait until it was over. But I couldn't. The gladiators were fighting for their lives. Some were fighting to honour their gods. Others were fighting because winning could set them free or grant them a pardon. Most had no choice. The masses were there to watch so that the common mortal could come face-to-face with death, see it as it was, and exorcise some of the horror. Death had less power over those who could confront it. Death had no power over those who laughed at it. In the stands, the people settled back in their seats and some opened bags of food. Others chatted or commented on the moves the fighters were making.

A gladiator dodged a deadly thrust and parried with his sword and the crowd nearby cheered. The sound raised my hackles. The slither and clang of iron and bronze weapons hitting each other were sharp, amplified by the stone walls.

Two men were practically at our feet. At equal distances around the circle, the groups of men sought footing in the deep sand and soon their laboured breathing sounded like dogs barking. The two fighters beneath us were evenly matched. One had red hair and the tattoos of a barbarian from the northern woods, like Oppi, and one was an Iberian warrior with hair spiked with chalk and his chest in painted red, black, and white concentric circles. Each wore bronze Phrygian helmets, shin guards with kneecap protection, and arm guards on their left arms. They wore leather skirts with high waistbands for extra protection. However, their chests, backs, necks, thighs, and right shoulders were bare. That made a fair number of targets, and soon the men were bleeding freely, scarlet ribbons of blood running down their legs and arms.

The redheaded man took a clanging blow on the head and he staggered, bracing himself with his sword so as not to fall. I uttered a shocked cry, clutching Plexis on the arm, but the Iberian didn't press his advantage because he'd received a fist-full of sand in his eyes. There was a lull in the fight as the two men circled each other warily. They had been pressing for an advantage, but neither found a chink in the other's defences.

Scorching sun beat mercilessly down on the fighters, and on the other side of the arena a shout went up as one gladiator pinned another to the ground with his trident. There was an expectant pause while the man holding the trident looked up at the public. If they waved their handkerchiefs his adversary was spared, if they held their thumbs down he was doomed.

The silence lasted a few minutes. It was the first life-or-death choice, and the people weren't ready. The thirst for blood had not taken its hold. Soon it would grow until it could not be slaked, and that was when the Game of Phersu would start. But for now, the crowd was just getting in the mood. After a slight hesitation, the people in front of the fighters held their thumbs down, but it was more to protest against the poor fighting of the loser than anything else. With a curt nod, the gladiator thrust his trident down and the first combatant died in quick, thrashing silence. For the men, if they could, avoided causing needless suffering. They expected the same courtesy from their adversaries.

From my seat, I didn't see the gladiator die, because the action had taken place on the far side of the bonfire. I could only see the head and shoulders of the man still standing. Then the clowns rushed over and took the loser's body away.

They propped him up and made it seem as if the dead body walked. With shouts and jeers they took his arms and draped them over their shoulders, making the body appear drunk. With exaggerated gestures, they took off his helmet and armour, then waltzed the body to the funeral pyre, which was burning hotly in the centre of the arena. They made a mockery of the priest's ceremony, pouring the wine down their own throats instead of onto the body. They tossed the roasted barley into the air and snapped at it with their long teeth, for some wore the masks of dogs and others wore the disguise of pigs with long tusks.

Then the gladiator who'd won came and made a show of chasing the demons away. The crowd roared, screaming curses at the costumed demons and throwing rotten fruit and vegetables at them. The gladiator motioned to the priests, and the dead man had a proper ceremony after all, before his body was disposed upon the pyre.

The fighting continued. A grim determination animated the gladiators. The crowd in the stands started shouting encouragement at their favourites. The mood of the public began to swing from nervousness to excitement. Hysteria was slowly building. Beneath the bleachers, the slaves stood and watched, their gaming forgotten, their eyes glittering strangely in the deep shadows.

I tried to wrench my gaze from the two men fighting at our feet. The sound of their breathing and grunts as they gave and received glancing blows horrified me. I looked at Plexis, wondering what he thought of the whole thing. He was sitting back in his seat, a stunned expression upon his face.

'What is it?' I asked.

'In Greece, the games are for proving athletic prowess, they are not bloody massacres. I had begun to think the Romans were like us, civilized, but I see they are not. They are the worst barbarians I've ever seen.' His voice was tight – he spoke through clenched teeth. I was glad he was whispering; Romans surrounded us, leaning forward, shouting and encouraging the atrocity. I thought of Alexander down in the arena and shuddered.

'Paul, are you all right?' I asked him, touching his shoulder.

He turned and nodded mutely. His lips were white, his eyes bleak. Then he hunched his shoulders and turned back towards the ring.

The afternoon wore on, the ringing of metal upon metal setting my teeth on edge and abrading my nerves. Another gladiator fell and the crowd howled. He died kicking, with blood spurting from his neck. There was the same silence afterwards; the same pause while the clowns had a mock fight with the priests for the fighter's body. Then the fighting began anew, and the gladiators seemed galvanized, somehow. Their movements were faster, the swords met with the sound of clanging, and the crowd screamed encouragement.

In front of us, the Iberian suddenly got lucky and found an opening in his adversary's defences. He lunged, stabbing the redheaded man in the groin. A fountain of blood confirmed his fate. The Iberian grinned wolfishly, his shoulders suddenly squaring. The other man knew he was doomed. He kept to his feet, somehow, staggering. In his

161

pale blue eyes was the haunted look of a fox caught in a trap. He bowed his head and held his shield low, hiding the wound from sight, but the sand beneath him turned scarlet. The Iberian stepped back, waiting. He knew it was only a matter of time. They circled each other, the Iberian on the outside. He was forcing the other man to move, to follow him, parrying his sharp thrusts.

I was crying. I couldn't help it. My nose was bleeding and tears were practically blinding me, but I couldn't tear my eyes from the ring. The scent of blood and urine was overpowering. In front of me, the three boys sat without moving. They were hardly breathing. Not one of us moved except Phaleria, who uttered a choked sound and hid her face in Demos's shoulder.

It was soon over. The redheaded man grew progressively paler. Sweat stood out on his brow, his face became ashen and he had to use his shield as a crutch to hold himself upright. He tried to parry another blow, and took a cut on the arm. The pain made him vomit, or it may have been dizziness from loss of blood. He retched, all the while keeping his face and shield turned towards the Iberian. There was a lull in the fighting when another gladiator screamed and fell not too far away. The cheers of the crowd distracted the two men. The Iberian went so far as to turn in the direction of the clamour. I thought the redheaded barbarian would take advantage of his opponent's inattention to attack, but he was dying, and he knew it. There was no need to take his adversary with him. Perhaps they had been combat partners in the training school. Perhaps they were friends. Whatever the reason, he simply waited, staring at the sky, while the crowd and the Iberian concentrated on the scene nearby.

When the Iberian turned again, his opponent was still standing. He looked perplexed for a moment; he must have thought the other man would be lying on the sand by now. There was no help for it; he would have to administer the *coup de grâce*. He drew a deep breath and uttered the first war cry we'd heard that day. The battle cry of the fierce Iberians, a cry that raised gooseflesh up and down my back and made my hair stand on end.

There was a hush in the crowd after the cry echoed eerily around the arena, and every head swivelled our way.

The Iberian uttered his whooping screams, battering his opponent with his heavy sword, his face a frozen mask of dementia as the lust for blood suddenly hit him. The redheaded man gamely lifted his shield, but his sword wavered. He made a feeble attempt to ward off the blows that rained down upon him. Then he moved his shield to one side.

I don't know if anyone noticed what happened next. If you weren't right in front, as we were, I think the scene would have appeared differently. But I saw, and Plexis, who was a swordsman, suddenly drew his breath with a sharp whistle. The redheaded man moved his shield and tilted his head to one side. The Iberian hesitated. He paused, just a fraction of a second, and in that moment his face changed. He lost his madness. He lost his crazed look, and he struck the redheaded man squarely on his exposed neck.

The redheaded man had bared his own neck to end his suffering. He couldn't endure any more, and crumpled at the Iberian's feet without a sound. The Iberian threw his weapons to the ground and knelt next to his adversary. I couldn't see his face; his back was to us, but I could hear his entreaties. I didn't speak his language, but I got the gist of what he was saying. He was begging the other man's forgiveness. I couldn't take a breath without gasping. Shuddering, I pressed my handkerchief to my nose and watched as the clowns drew near, but they didn't get close to the fallen gladiator. The Iberian stood up suddenly, his sword in hand, and threatened the clowns. He wouldn't let them take the body away to defile it with mockery. Instead, he gathered his opponent's body in his arms and carried him to the funeral pyre. He scattered the barley over the corpse and poured the sacred wine onto the dead man. He drew off his opponent's armour, pausing when he came to the helmet. Hardly anyone was looking. They were watching the other combats around the ring. The end was drawing near for several gladiators. Blood was flowing freely from many wounds; there were viscous pools of it on the ground. The pale sand was streaked and splattered with scarlet.

The Iberian was alone in the centre of the ring with his rival's body. He carefully removed the helmet, smoothing stray locks of bright hair from the blanched face. Then he leaned down and kissed him. It looked as if he whispered in his ear. Next, he laid the body on the funeral pyre, stepping back quickly and rubbing his singed arms. The smoke roiled, billowed, and rose towards the heavens. The Iberian raised his face to the sky, and watched the smoke. His face was inscrutable. Had he lost a friend or an enemy? It didn't seem to matter. He watched the smoke rise to the heavens, contemplating the path souls took as they left this earthly realm.

When the last fight finished, abruptly, there was an expectant rustling in the crowd. The people were tense; a shiver ran through the air. The gladiators who'd triumphed, and the clowns, huddled together, all differences between costumed demon and gladiator forgotten. The sun touched the horizon and slid behind it. Deep shadows gobbled up the arena, and the funeral pyre cast a perfect circle of orange light upon the sand. It was almost burned down. Only an enormous heap of glowing embers and charred bones remained, with an occasional tongue of flame licking towards the sky.

The puddles of blood turned black, the white glare of the sun on the sand disappeared. Everything was grey and muted. The colours became monochrome in the blue evening air. The air grew suddenly cooler. With a loud crash, the huge bronze doors guarding the entrance leading into the heart of the hillside, flew open. Inside was pitch-black. The silence grew. Everyone craned forward, but their faces were strained, nervous. There were fearful looks. The Phersu was coming. The Game of Phersu was about to begin.

Chapter Ten

There was no clash of cymbals this time, no blare of trumpets announcing the demon's arrival. In silence, he strode lightly out of the darkness, picking his way almost delicately past the blood on the ground. He traipsed towards the centre of the ring, standing near, but not quite within, the circle of light. He bowed to the four sides of the arena, but his bow was not met with the jeers and cheers the other clown demons had elicited. Instead, his cavorting was met with a watchful stillness.

The Phersu wore strange garb, almost, but not quite, like the Harlequin of the future. He had the same black and white diamond patterned jacket and knickers and the same pointed hat with a red pom-pom bouncing gaily on its pinnacle. He wore a black mask, under which a white face could just be glimpsed. His mouth was wide and painted very red, and he never showed his teeth. In my mind they were pointed like little needles. My imagination attributed him a shark's blank-eyed expression. Plexis reached down and sought my hand. He grasped my false hand and jumped, startled enough to utter a little cry. Then he grinned ruefully at me and wiped a bead of sweat off his brow. We sat on the edge of our seats. I swallowed and took his hand with my right hand. Our palms were slick with perspiration.

The clown bowed one last time then clapped his hands sharply. The sound echoed like a shot, and they led Alexander out of the dark doorway. Four soldiers escorted him. He was wearing nothing but a short, pleated skirt. His arms were tied behind his back. I had thought that he would be blindfolded, as the game required, but thankfully, he was not. No hood covered his bright hair and no mask hid his parti-coloured eyes.

'Why isn't his face covered?' I managed to whisper.

Demos answered in a monotone. 'We paid the *lanista*. Plus, I think they want the crowd to see him. Otherwise, it could be anyone beneath the mask.'

Alexander walked as lightly as the demon had. This gave the crowd pause. Even the demon Phersu stopped gesturing and cocked his head. There was nothing in Alexander's demeanour that gave the least indication of alarm. He was led to the circle of firelight, and then the soldiers stepped back. Each held a long rope; they were attached to Alexander's ankles. And his arms, besides being fastened behind his back, had ropes tied just above his elbows. Alexander didn't move. He stood in the firelight and waited. His hair glittered and his skin shone. Oil covered his body – the slick oil was his only defence. The Phersu bowed to him, tauntingly, and he bowed back.

That, too, made the Phersu hesitate. It was ever so slight, but my heightened senses perceived it. Everything seemed to be moving in slow motion. A flame leapt up brightly, the air was as clear as a magnifying glass, and the faces of everyone in the arena were painfully distinct. I clenched my hand, making Plexis wince. In front of me, Paul stiffened, and Scipio began to mutter strange incantations in a low, furious whisper. Hirkan hesitated, then joined him, their voices weaving in the evening air.

The soldiers handed the ends of their ropes to the Phersu. He wound them around his hand, making a great show of it, while Alexander stood in front of him, immobile. He wore an insolent look on his face as he stared at the demon. The demon stared back at him, his eyes two black holes in his mask, his mouth frozen in spite.

Plexis breathed in painful gulps. I couldn't disengage my hand from his to touch Paul on the shoulder, and I couldn't turn my head to see if Plexis was all right. My whole being was focused on the scene in front of me.

The four soldiers left the arena, and the rest of the clowns and the gladiators followed in silence. The Phersu was alone with Alexander and, for the first time, he spoke. His voice rang out, high and hysterical in its fervour and brilliance.

'Welcome to the Game of Phersu!' he screamed. 'The Great Alexander has returned from the Underworld to compete in our arena! Let Cerberus come and take him back again! His shade has no business in the world of the living!'

The crowd shook off its impassivity and screamed, urging the Phersu to call Cerberus, the hound that guarded the gates of Hades.

The Phersu pretended to consider, tilting his head to one side and prancing back and forth. He tugged at the leashes binding Alexander, trying to unbalance him, but my husband was as quick as a cat, using his formidable coordination to stay upright and to appear nonchalant. The crowd howled its approval, and the Phersu bowed in mocking appreciation. He tossed all but one leash to the ground and raised one arm above his head. When he snapped his fingers another door opened, and a shadow slunk out.

I choked back a cry. It was a huge, black dog. The animal was as large as a bear, with the long muzzle of a wolf and the broad head and muscled jaws of a mastiff. Covered in rough fur, he wore a metal collar with sharp spikes. The beast was acting strangely. Instead of a dog's quick trot, he slunk. His head swung back and forth, his nose twitched, and white froth dripped from his gaping jaws.

'What is the matter with him?' Paul asked, twisting around and looking at us with wide eyes. 'Why is the dog behaving that way? Is he mad?'

Demos answered, 'He's been drugged to make him more aggressive. He isn't rabid, that would be too dangerous for everyone.'

The animal circled the edges of the arena, his gait slow, but determined. Every now and then, he would stop and snarl at nothing, his teeth snapping ferociously at thin air, his hackles raised. Neither Alexander nor the Phersu moved a muscle. The dog had almost completed his circle, when something burst in the fire sending a popping shower of sparks into the air. The dog spun around, barking and snapping at the sudden movement. He attacked a shadow

169

then, leaping on it and finding a pool of blood. He howled in rage, rushing back and forth through the blood, teeth clicking madly together, glittering in the firelight. Then he stopped and began his deliberate search again. It didn't take long for him to catch the scent of the two men standing near the fire. He crouched low, muzzle in the air, his lips drawn back in a silent snarl. Alexander didn't move. I saw his eyes gleam, though, as he turned his head slightly.

The Phersu stayed immobile. He stood, arms crossed, as if he were at a garden party waiting for a glass of champagne. Then he gave a vehement tug at the rope, causing Alexander to shift his balance. That was the stimulus the dog needed. He gathered himself and launched his huge body at the puny human helpless before him.

Or not so helpless. Alexander waited until the colossus was nearly upon him before rolling onto his back. With his legs, he caught the dog under the belly lifting him up and over his head and tossing him into the bonfire behind him.

The dog disappeared in a shower of red sparks, but he shot out instantaneously, screeching in pain, his fur smouldering. He rolled in the sand, then stood squarely again, snarling mistrustfully at his prey. This time he didn't rush in. He feinted, waiting for Alexander to drop to the ground again. Instead, Alexander jumped backwards out of range of the snapping jaws. He would have escaped unscathed from that attack, but the Phersu jerked on the ropes that held him and he stumbled. The dog managed to sink his teeth into his calf, but Alexander was moving too fast and the beast didn't get a good grip. Flesh tore, though, and the dog stood a moment and licked fresh blood from his muzzle, a weird growl vibrating in the air.

I uttered a low sob and Paul cried out, but his voice was lost in the roar of the crowd as they screamed for blood, more blood.

Alexander stood, his legs braced, and for the first time, he looked directly at the Phersu. His lips were moving, but I don't know what he was saying. He held his head low, like a bull about to charge, and the Phersu took an involuntary step backwards. The dog was upon the Phersu in a second. Movement was all the beast needed to spur an attack. The Phersu easily evaded the sharp teeth, and as he dodged, he gave a mighty pull on the leashes, forcing Alexander to follow him. Ungainly, bound and hampered, Alexander looked easy prey. However, the dog missed again when he leapt at Alexander, and the crowd's howls grew in volume until the stadium trembled.

The dog's next attack was more careful, and the Phersu gave a pernicious tug at the ropes as Alexander tried to twist sideways. His arms, fastened behind his back, made his balance precarious. Alexander came away with a chunk torn out of his thigh and slashes under his ribs. Fresh blood ran from his wounds, exciting the dog even more. I saw Alexander's muscles tense as he waited for another attack.

My heart was hammering wildly. Blood trickled from my nose and my eyes stung with tears. The man I loved more than my life was being torn to pieces while I watched, and I could do nothing to help him. If I'd had the strength, I would have left the arena, I couldn't bear it any longer, but I was paralyzed with horror.

Plexis could hardly breathe. Each time he drew a breath, it sounded like a sharp gasp. We sat with our trembling shoulders pressed together, our gazes riveted to the ghastly scene before us, waiting for the inevitable end. In front of us, Scipio and Hirkan kept up their whispered chanting while Paul sobbed bitterly, his body shaking.

Alexander staggered, his hands still fastened behind his back, trying to keep his feet underneath him while the Phersu yanked at the ropes. The dog darted in and out again trying to hamstring his weakening quarry. The beast was confident now, sure of the outcome. Alexander bled from many wounds. The Phersu had reverted to the motionless statue he had been before, only moving his hands to twitch the ropes. His eyes glittered when his victim stumbled, but otherwise he showed no emotion.

Despite his injuries and the apparent hopelessness of the situation, Alexander didn't look frightened. His expression grave, he concentrated upon the dog's savage strikes, but there was no panic in his movements. I thought it very strange, until I noticed that he'd worked one hand free.

Demos's shout catapulted us out of our seats. Phaleria took her hands away from her face to look, and I gave a cry of amazement. Alexander was holding a short blade. I don't know where it came from, but it took only a moment to cut himself free of the binding ropes.

The Phersu was astounded. He hurled the ropes to the ground and uttered an outraged shriek. Alexander paid no attention, he was busy dodging another determined assault from the hellhound, but now he was unhindered, and now he was armed.

He and the dog circled each other on equal footing. The crowd hushed, everyone stood or leaned forward, intent on the two figures in the dusk.

They appeared to dance. The shadows grew longer as the fire burned down. The embers cast a scarlet light on Alexander's slick skin and the dog's matted fur. They looked like two demons capering on the bone-white sand. The dog's attacks became less frenzied and more calculated. The knife in Alexander's hand flashed in the firelight as he held the beast at bay.

The crowd lost its hysteria. A supernatural quiet fell over the gathering and deepened with the blue shadows. I could hear my heartbeat, the whisper of the sand beneath Alexander's feet, and the sound of the dog's teeth as they snapped together. I don't know how long the fight lasted. Perhaps only minutes, although it seemed like hours. Time slowed, the air stilled, the two figures converged in one of the deeper shadows, and only one came out again. It advanced painfully, crawling, to collapse in front of the red embers.

My breath caught in my throat. In front of me, Paul's shoulders twitched sharply, but neither of us uttered a sound. For a heart-stopping second I'd thought it was the dog, but no, it was Alexander on his hands and knees.

He crouched, gathering his strength, and then rose to his feet. Pale sand and black blood streaked his body. Burnished red by the dying incandescence of the embers, he frightened me more than he ever had. His eyes were enormous, his face haggard, and his chest heaved. Then he tilted his head to the side, a gesture I knew so well, and I let

173

my breath out in a long shuddering sigh. Next to me, Plexis stirred like a branch in the wind, and we clutched each other, two people drowning in a roaring sea of acclamations. The crowd voiced its approbation while Alexander stood in the middle of the applause and marshalled his strength. He held his head high. He ignored the blood streaming from his wounds, but he didn't try to walk. His legs were braced beneath him; I could tell it was an effort for him to stand.

I looked for the Phersu, but he had vanished. One moment he was standing next to the smouldering remains of a fire, the next instant he was gone. A wisp of grey smoke wafted across the sand. Then a breeze picked it up and whirled it away. Silent as shadows amidst the wild cheering, the gladiators came back into the arena for the final parade.

They lifted Alexander, holding him above their heads. Arms reached down from the stands as the people tried to touch him. Over and over, they chanted his name as the parade marched around the ring. The costumed demons joined the parade, but they were defeated now. They slunk in the back of the procession while the crowd booed and jeered at them. The Phersu never reappeared. I searched for him, my heart hammering painfully, but he was gone, vanquished, extinguished.

Two strong men slung the dog's huge carcass between them. They held the beast's legs over their shoulders and its muzzle and tail trailed on the ground. Its jaws gaped open, revealing sharp teeth. The spectators shrank back with shrill cries of fright when it passed.

For Alexander, there was nothing but adulation. Flowers and coins rained down upon him. The gladiators waved at the crowd, but Alexander was unmoving. He was in pain. His injuries were grave and I could hear Demos muttering angrily. I hoped that Axiom, who was waiting at the villa, would have the medicine he needed for Alexander's wounds. I hoped that Augustus would have his chariot ready to take Alexander back to the villa as quickly as possible. The procession drew near. Alexander searched the crowd with his gaze, and when he saw us, he smiled. His eyes were illuminated with a fierce light. Otherwise, he held himself painfully still. I didn't dare wave, although the three boys were leaning forwards, ecstatically calling out his name. Paul's voice was broken, hoarse with screaming. Phaleria sobbed and waved her scarf above her head, while Demos's bellows made the air around us tremble. Plexis and I hunkered in our seats, holding each other tightly, tears in our eyes. I was still shaking, Plexis tried to ease my hand from his arm, but I was clutching too tightly; I wouldn't let go. I had been too frightened.

If what Demos said was right, then Alexander would first go into the gladiators' quarters where a doctor would examine him. I didn't know if the doctors would be any good, although Demos told me that the gladiators had the best physicians available. I wanted to go to Alexander, however only men or slaves were allowed into the rooms and corridors beneath the Circus Maximus.

Chapter Eleven

We went to Augustus's villa. He'd come with three chariots, enough to carry us all. Alexander, he informed us, would come later that evening when the doctors finished with him. Plexis stayed behind.

Elaina took my arm and led me away. I was reluctant to go, but my legs quivered and I felt light-headed. I realized that I hadn't eaten anything for over a day. I shook my head and tried to concentrate on what Elaina was saying, but instead my eyes drifted to my son, who was speaking to Demos. Paul gazed at the big man and his face was hard. I'd rarely seen him wear that expression. I thought I knew what they were discussing though. It turned out I was right. Demos wanted to find the glass merchant's slave.

The three boys chattered all the way back to the country villa, their faces flushed and their voices high with excitement. I recognized Paul's hectic mood. Alexander was often like that after a battle. All the emotions mixed with relief were letting themselves out in a rush. Hirkan and Scipio were standing together in the chariot, their arms linked for balance. Their bodies were pressed shoulder to shoulder, heads touching and coming apart as they spoke, laughed, and jested. I wondered, vaguely ill at ease, if the boys would turn to each other sexually. I was used to such scenes after following Alexander's army for ten years; but I wasn't sure if ten years old was the right age to be initiated into such rites. Scipio and Hirkan were both older. I gripped the side of the chariot as we rode on, turning an attentive face towards Elaina. I would insist Paul stay with me for the night.

Her voice snapped me out of my thoughts.

'Of course, when we heard that your husband was the Great Iskander, we wondered if it were a farce. He couldn't have come back from the dead, no one does. You realize that since his death, several imposters have participated in the Game of Phersu, but your husband was the first to survive. Now, I'm sure, the gladiator guild will want to keep him on. Why, he could make a fortune! The *lanista* will offer him a considerable sum. If he insists on pretending to be the Great Iskander, however, he will have to fight battles that are even more difficult. I think you should be aware of that.'

For a moment I was at a loss for words, then I nodded slowly. 'I was hoping, actually, that your husband could help us,' I said.

She smiled. 'After you saved Scipio, I'm sure there's nothing we can refuse you.'

I didn't tell her that Scipio had been endangered solely by my own thoughtless actions. Instead, I thanked her and told her I wanted to move Paul's bed into my room for the night.

At the villa, Axiom was waiting impatiently to greet us. He had heard the news of Alexander's victory from one of Augustus's messenger pigeons. Still, I thought he appeared extremely worried as he helped Elaina and me out of the chariot.

I asked Elaina if she could have food sent up to my room. Then Axiom, Paul, and I went to join Yovanix, who was waiting for us.

Paul was still frantic with excitement, tripping over his tongue in his haste to describe the fight. Axiom and Yovanix listened to the recital, now and then asking a question, but otherwise silent. Axiom was more shocked than Yovanix about the gladiators. Yovanix had been a slave in Massalia, a port frequented by the Romans. He'd heard about their games, and had even witnessed such things as cockfights and bear-baiting. Axiom was profoundly disquieted after hearing about Alexander's wounds. He got up and paced, nearly colliding with the slave bringing us a huge tray of food.

Yovanix and Paul sat on the floor, and Paul served Yovanix his dinner, telling him what everything was on his plate, while Axiom and I spoke in worried whispers.

'I want to leave Rome as soon as possible, before Alexander truly gets recognized and made a permanent fixture in the games,' I said to Axiom. 'I wanted to go to Pompeii, but now I'm not sure if it's a good idea. The Romans' idea of entertainment is a ghastly, bloody, parody of sport.' I was badly shaken.

'I agree. It's too dangerous now. Even if he's not recognized, the fact that he won the Game of Phersu means every *lanista* will want to recruit him.' Axiom rubbed his face. 'It's good thing he had a knife. I wonder where he got it.'

'Maybe a gladiator dropped it in the sand, and he found it.' I'd wondered the same thing, but thinking about the fight made my heart pound. I felt sick and pushed my plate away.

'Here, take this,' said Axiom, passing me a glass vial with a clear, amber liquid in it.

'What is it? Will it hurt the baby?' I asked. 'I don't want any drugs.'

'Don't worry. Vix made it. I promise it won't hurt you or the babe. But you need it.' He pressed it into my hand. 'It will blunt the edge of your shock and help you sleep. I must go and prepare medicine for Alexander.'

I sipped the bitter brew while Paul ate, talked, and gestured, reliving the whole battle several times. His words became muffled as my head swam. *I need to lie down*, I thought to myself.

I don't remember falling asleep. I woke up next day groggy, my head aching as if from a hangover, and my mouth dry. Then I remembered the sleeping draught. It had been a strong one, prepared by Vix. I blinked, then sat up. I was not alone in the room. Axiom, Yovanix, and Plexis were sitting on the rug. A breakfast platter of fresh fruit and smoked meats was on a table. And lying quite still, in a narrow bed near the window, was Alexander. His face was turned away from me, so I didn't know if he was awake or not. Plexis and Axiom were whispering.

Then Plexis noticed me, rose and came silently over to me. He sank down on the bed and put a hand on my shoulder. I felt his fingers tighten on my collarbone then relax, like a tremor. 'Do you want some fruit?' he asked quietly, motioning towards the tray set on the low table next to Axiom.

'Yes. Is he all right?' I asked, looking at Alexander.

Plexis didn't look at me. His hand tightened again. 'He needs rest. The doctors at the Circus are very capable. They treated his wounds with alum and cauterized the worst ones. He'll limp even more now, but his hamstring wasn't damaged. He'll be sore for a few days, but I suppose he's used to that.' He spoke in a low voice, more a murmur really, but Alexander had ears like a bat.

'Do you really think I'm used to being hurt?' he asked, turning to face us. His eyes were sunken and his face lined with fatigue. 'I wish I *were* used to it, then perhaps it wouldn't pain me so much.'

'You're awake!' I got out of bed and knelt at his side. 'You scared me so much,' I told him, taking his hand and pressing it to my mouth.

'I promise, by Mars and Jupiter, that I will never take part in another Roman game.'

'By Mars and Jupiter? What happened to Ares and Zeus? Are you becoming Roman?' Plexis frowned at his friend.

'No, but when in Rome ...' his voice trailed off. We sat in silence, our hands entwined. Then he sighed, shifted on his pallet, and winced. 'I was lucky, you realize. When I was captured, I didn't understand at first. Then, when I was

180

taken to the Circus Maximus, I *thought* I knew what would happen. But nothing I have ever seen or heard about prepared me for the Game of Phersu.'

'How did you get the knife?' I wanted to know.

'Ahh, that was part of the luck I was speaking of. When I was inside the Circus, I met the gladiators and one of them was a man who'd fought in my army. He recognized me, but didn't say anything to anyone else. He slipped me the knife just before I was taken to my prison cell. I never saw him again, so I suppose he was defeated in the arena.' He was silent a moment, thinking, then he sighed. 'He was a good man. I would have liked to have been able to repay him. He gave me the knife that saved me. Otherwise, I would never have been able to sever my bonds and kill the beast.'

'Did anyone else recognize you?' I pressed.

'No.' His voice was dry. 'Fear not, for your Time-Gods will not find any trace of me here. The Circus has had many Alexanders. I was but one in a crowd.'

'I wasn't thinking of that.'

His face relaxed, seeing my distress. 'I'm sorry. It's just nerves.'

'We're all on edge,' said Axiom. 'I'll be glad to leave this city.'

Alexander shivered. 'I thought, in the beginning, that Rome was like Greece. But it isn't. It is a mockery of Greece, a nightmare of Athens. The strangeness of the Etruscans seeps through to the surface and troubles the reflection of Roman civilization. The people sitting in the stands are more barbaric than the tattooed men who fight in their arena. They dress in fine robes, eat delicate meats, and live in houses that boast plumbing and heating, yet they are savages. Do you remember once, Ashley, you wondered what would have happened if the Romans had been beaten by the Greeks? What would have happened if I had conquered the Gauls, and not them? I wonder now myself what would have transpired.'

'Perhaps the world would have been more civilized,' I said. 'Where is Paul? Has he eaten breakfast?'

'Yes, don't worry about him. He's gone to find his friends. Tell me, why did he sleep here last night, and not with them?' Alexander asked, then he winced when he tried to shift his position in bed. 'I hurt everywhere. I knew there was a reason I fearedbig dogs.' He shuddered. 'Although I strongly doubt that was a dog. I'm willing to bet it came directly from Hades.'

'Like yourself,' I said.

'Very funny. Why did Paul sleep here?'

I honestly didn't know what to answer, and I was saved from doing so by the boy in question, who poked his head into the room and asked in a loud whisper, 'Is Father awake yet?'

'He is, and you can see him. But don't jostle him, he's still in pain,' said Axiom, measuring powder into a cup of wine then stirring it.

'Hirkan and Scipio want to see him too.'

'Bring them in,' said Plexis, lifting me to my feet and settling me comfortably on a low couch. He gave me a plate of food and practically fed it to me while the three boys crowded reverently around Alexander, bending as close to him as Axiom would allow, and peppering him with questions.

'Is it true that you are the Great Iskander?' Scipio wanted to know. 'And if it's true, will you teach me the art of war? I need to learn in order to destroy Carthage and avenge my father.'

I started at that, but Plexis pressed another piece of melon into my hand and said, 'Eat!'

Hirkan wanted to know if the dog really had been Cerberus, because, he added ingenuously, 'If you are the Great Conqueror come back from Hades, you'd certainly have recognized the hellhound.'

Paul wanted to know if Alexander would get the beast's pelt, because he wanted to show it to Chiron. He also wanted a few of its teeth to put on a necklace like the ones the Iberian warriors wore.

I stood up and slipped out of the room while Alexander answered the boys' questions. I wanted to bathe, and I wanted to speak to Elaina. All I could think about was getting out of Rome. Too many people knew about Alexander. The threat of being erased would always hang over my head like Damocles' sword. I hated living with the fear, but I had learned to accept it, as I'd learned to accept my missing hand. Yet, sometimes I reached for things, forgetting it was no longer part of me, and sometimes I could relax and forget about the future. When I remembered, it always startled me. I couldn't let my guard down.

Elaina was in the kitchen, overseeing her slaves. She held an enormous eel in her hands and she was explaining to a young man how to prepare it. 'After you remove the skin you must cut it in even pieces. Then, soak it in a mixture of fresh rabbit's blood and honey. Add a handful of thyme and a cup of vinegar. You leave it overnight and in the morning pat the eel dry and cook it in hot olive oil. Brown it well on every side, then put it in the stew pot with three cups of wine, one half cup of honey, three cloves of garlic, a pinch of salt, and a pitcher of well water. When it has boiled, add the marinade, cover it, and cook it slowly for five hours.' She handed the eel to the cook, who took it gingerly. Elaina saw me and smiled.

'Just a moment, I must wash my hands.' Elaina motioned to a slave holding a brass bowl. She rinsed her hands in the lemon-scented water and wrinkled her nose. 'Nothing gets the odour of eel out, except lots of lemon. Do you like to cook?' she asked.

'I never learned how,' I admitted.

'I was taught by my mother. She made sure I studied the culinary arts. I prefer cooking to weaving,' she said, shrugging.

'I wanted to thank you for your hospitality and beg a favour of you.'

'Go ahead, ask me anything.' She rubbed her hands briskly and watched, her eyes narrowed, as a slave began to skin a rabbit.

'I want to leave today. Could you ask your husband to make sure the proper passes are ready?'

'Of course. You are heading towards Pompeii, are you not? I shall be sorry to see you go,' said Elaina, surprising me. 'I wanted to ask you so many things; you have travelled so far and seen so much. I have gone to Gaul as far as our farm in the Rhone valley and south as far as Carthage once. But I've never seen Athens or been to Iberia. Is Athens as lovely as they say? What did you appreciate the most? Have you been to Babylon? Tell me about it, please? Are the gardens fully as wonderful as they say?'

I shivered at the mention of that city. The name would always prickle the hair on the back of my neck. 'I was in Babylon, yes, and the Hanging Gardens were incredible.' She took my arm and led me to the garden. We strolled through the shade of the yew trees while I told her about the gardens and the great palace. Then I described Athens as best I could. I had been there once, but three thousand years in the future, and the buildings I'd seen had been in ruins, so I had to embroider. I told her the nicest city I'd seen so far had been Alexandria, but that Rome was a lovely place also. Iberia was quite savage, I assured her, with hardly any proper cities. Parisii was an interesting town, and if she wanted, she should go to Glanum or Massalia to buy wonderful soap and perfumes.

Elaina listened avidly. As I've already said, people loved to get news and hear descriptions of far-off places. They were thirsty for stories, songs and news. Travellers were welcome in private homes – they were expected to entertain with gossip. I tried to be as interesting as possible, knowing that Elaina would appreciate my stories as much as if I'd given her a new book to read or a picture. I finished describing the jewellery and clothes I'd seen in the North. Then I tried to remember a recipe for octopus stew I'd eaten in Iberia.

185

When the sun grew hot, I begged her leave and went to pack our belongings. Alexander was sleeping when I went into the room. Plexis was off somewhere with Augustus, and Axiom was with Paul. Silently, I put my toilet articles in my small, sandalwood chest. Alexander had given the chest to me in Arbeles, ten years ago. The wood was polished smooth, and the brass clasp was shiny with use. I closed it slowly, then sank down on my bed and held my face in my hand. A great lassitude came over me. I sat there until a small flutter in my stomach startled me. The baby was starting to kick. He was growing. I smiled and put my hand over my belly. The bump was getting bigger; I looked like I had a melon under my robe. Tears suddenly rolled down my cheeks. The stress and anguish of yesterday were catching up on me. I sat on my bed and shook. My teeth chattered. I tried to stop them but couldn't. Alexander rolled over and opened his eyes. They were sunken with pain, shadowed with fatigue, but still magnificent. He raised himself up on his elbow and motioned to me.

'Come here,' he ordered.

I obeyed. My legs trembled when I walked, but I made it to his bed. He reached up and pulled me to him. We lay on the bed and he undressed me, his hands urgent. His mouth was urgent as well, seeking my lips, my breasts, my throat. He rolled over and pinned me beneath him. There were no words between us. None were needed. There was just the harsh sound of his breathing, my low moans, and the steady creak, creak, of the bed beneath us.

Chapter Twelve

I was glad to leave Rome. All its rules and regulations were just a thin veneer of civilization hiding the most ruthless, bloodthirsty people I'd met so far. The Romans would have been horrified to hear of themselves described in those terms. They considered their city the most civilized place on earth, and their rules and regulations were proof of their superiority. I thought that the Game of Phersu was proof enough of their barbarism. But when the boat left the harbour and we sailed down river, I couldn't help looking back at the city with something like a pang of homesickness. It was odd, but only Rome had resembled the cities I'd known in the future: the dilapidated apartment buildings hung with laundry, the traffic jams, the bossy police, the tourists gawking, and even the stadium.

Paul was glum; he hated leaving his new friends. Hirkan had insisted on staying with Scipio in Rome. Scipio had sworn undying friendship to Paul, promising letters every week, and to come to visit whenever he could. He gave Paul an amulet made of glass. It was a round pendant in the form of a bearded man's face. His eyes were round and staring, his beard was made of tiny, black glass beads. It was comical looking, but Scipio told Paul it was to protect him from evil. Evil covered quite a few things, from poison to lightning bolts, and Paul wore the pendant on a silken cord.

Augustus was anxious to visit us in Alexandria. With his Roman pragmatism, he'd already planned a trading voyage in the winter with produce from his farm in Gaul. Elaina had given me a farewell present. It was a Roman cookbook, handwritten on precious vellum. I was stunned. As we sailed away, I surprised myself by hoping I'd see her again soon. I would reciprocate with a gift of my own. Chirpa could help me compile a book of Greek, Persian, and Egyptian recipes. I looked at the first page of Elaina's cookbook – roasted wild boar chops with honey and thyme. It sounded delicious.

We left Rome in the morning and reached Pompeii, just down the coast, early the following afternoon. We didn't want to stay long, just enough time to pick up the money Ptolemy had we hoped – sent to the city. We were broke. The money Alexander had won in the Game of Phersu was gone. In a typical Alexander gesture, he'd given most of it to Hirkan to ensure that the boy would never become a slave or a gladiator. The rest he gave to Phaleria as payment for our voyage.

So now we had to go to a place called the 'Villa of the Faun' and pick up some gold.

We stayed there for three days. To Alexander's delight, there was a whole sack of mail. To my delight, the house was luxurious, with a shallow pool in the centre of the atrium. In the middle of the basin was a beautiful statue of a faun that gave the house its name. The house also boasted the famous mosaic, 'The Battle of Issus', in which Alexander had fought against Darius.

'That's an excellent likeness of Bucephalus', said Alexander as he leaned closer to examine the huge mosaic.

'It looks a great deal like Darius too,' said Axiom, standing back and squinting. His eyes had been bothering him for a while now, and I was afraid he had cataracts.

'But why did they make my nose so big?' asked Alexander, shaking his head.

'Your nose was broken then, don't you remember?' Axiom grinned. 'Look at that, your spear went right through the body of Darius's son-in-law. Poor fellow.'

'That must have hurt,' said Paul, whistling.

I was shocked. The mosaic was incredible; the fear in the dying man's face – he was little more than a chubby teenager – and the despair as Darius reached his hand out to save him was almost palpable. Around them, the fighting was intense. Alexander's face is stern and his eyes have an almost crazed look to them. I knew that look, having seen it several times before. The Phersu had taken a step backwards when he'd seen it. And I imagine that Darius knew the battle was lost as soon as he'd caught sight of those immense, parti-coloured eyes. He'd fled, leaving everything behind him, including his tent with his family huddled inside. His wives and children, and his mother, Sisygambis, became Alexander's prisoners.

Knowing the Persian protocol for their women, Alexander had made sure that no one entered the tent. He'd sent the family, under royal guard, back to their palace in Ecbatana, and never once did he try to catch a glimpse of

Darius's bride, the woman described as 'the most beautiful woman on earth'. I'd seen her, and it was true, she had been a bewitching beauty.

All those thoughts tumbled through my mind as I stared at the mosaic. Alexander was uncommonly silent as well. The dead tree in the picture, a real landmark in the actual battle, stretched bare branches to the lowering sky. There is no blue in this picture, only violent reds, oranges, browns, and the pitch-black of Darius's horse. There are splashes of white, Darius's robe and Alexander's spear glitter white. But the sky, Alexander's armour, and the tree are dark grey. The clouds are roiling, the winds of change are blowing, and two cultures have come in violent conflict.

'I won,' said Alexander, suddenly fierce.

We turned and stared at him. He was standing with his fists clenched and the skin around his nose and mouth had gone white.

'I won, and no one can take that away from me.' Then he left the room. In the three days that remained, I didn't see him there again. Although once, during the night, I woke up and he had gone. I didn't know where he went, but Axiom told me he'd seen a glow in that room, as if someone held a lamp.

We left Pompeii for another reason. The second day we were there, as we walked through the city, we turned a corner and came face-to-face with the insufferable Onesicrite.

I have no idea why he was there. He had been in Babylon when Alexander had died, and I thought I'd heard he'd gone back to Greece. But he hadn't. There he was, strolling down the street, looking into a bakery. When we saw him it was too late, he lifted his eyes, saw us, and turned purple.

He opened his mouth, like a fish, and started to gasp. He turned purple, then blue, and I remembered belatedly that the people of that time often carried their money around in their mouths. The silly goose was choking to death on an obol.

Well, it served him right. Demos, always glad for a new patient, leapt forward, grabbed Onesicrite and turned him upside down, while Axiom banged on his back. There was a hacking cough, a piece of silver shot out of his mouth, and Onesicrite sat down on the pavement and gaped at us.

'The Goddess!' he shrieked in a whisper. 'The Great and Mighty Iskander! You've come back from Hades' realm! Eeep! Eeep! It's the King of Heaven and Earth!'

Alexander winced; he'd always hated it when Onesicrite called him that.

For a minute, the only thing he could do was squeak, *eeep, eeep, eeep,* like a hysterical mouse, then Plexis strolled around the corner. 'Hephaestion! You died in Ecbatana!' Onesicrite's eyes rolled up in his head and he passed out, keeling over in the street.

'We can't leave him there,' said Axiom reasonably, as he dragged him out of the way of a chariot.

'Let's leave him over there in the shade,' I said nervously. 'Then we can get out of here.'

'What will happen when he wakes up and starts screaming?' asked Plexis, in an interested tone of voice.

'No one will believe him. If he said, "I saw the Great and Mighty Iskander", maybe some would believe. But he's going to be ranting about the goddess Persephone, Iskander, Hephaestion, and no one will take him seriously ever again.' Axiom was grinning.

I stared at the Greek journalist, lying in a heap. A giggle, albeit a nervous one, escaped me. I had always despised the fellow. He'd written the most biased accounts back to Greece, causing friction and discontent within the kingdom. After Alexander's death, the journalist had gone with Roxanne to Macedonia, but Cassander had thrown him out. That much we'd heard from a traveller in Rome. Now here he was, at my feet. My mouth curled in a grin. 'Well, it's about time no one took him seriously,' I said.

That was the last we saw of him, the last we ever heard about Onesicrite, Alexander's 'sex and scandal' journalist from Athens.

We finished our walk through the main part of town. We ended up at a racecourse where Alexander lost a great deal of money – most of it to a pickpocket and the rest betting on losing horses – and where Plexis won a great deal of money; he knew horses.

There were horse races and chariot races, and, as I said, thieves. They were everywhere, which was why people put their money in their mouths. The thieving guild was a very powerful one. It was perhaps the first organized labour union. The members paid dues, and there was a very strict hierarchy within the guild itself. The guild paid for lawyers when a thief was caught. It chipped in and took care of the widow and the orphans when the thief was found guilty –

despite the lawyer – and was sent to the mines, became a galley slave, or a permanent fixture in the gladiator games. Those were the punishments awaiting a criminal in those times, prisons not having been invented yet.

After the races, we wandered back to the Villa of the Faun, and waded in the pool to cool off. The weather was stifling hot – it was autumn, but a storm was brewing and the wind was from Africa. We would have to wait another day before setting sail. I was anxious to return to our home in Alexandria. I was impatient to see Chiron and Cleopatra again. I missed my two children so much.

That evening, Alexander shut himself in the bedroom and opened his mail while Plexis, Axiom, Paul, and I played dice games. Axiom frowned at the dice and then sat up and sighed. He rubbed a hand over his eyes and said, 'It's getting worse. I think I'll have to go see an eye doctor soon. Perhaps Usse can help me.'

I peered at his eyes and asked him to look towards the light. Faint clouds were visible when the firelight reflected from his irises a certain way. 'What can he do?' I asked.

'An operation,' Axiom sounded surprised. 'In your time, isn't there any cure for eye sickness?'

'Of course, but, we use lasers and can grow new lenses from a person's own cells. What do you do here?'

'We use a hollow needle and draw the sickness out. Usse will know what to do. The Gauls perfected the operation, but it was developed by the Egyptians.' Axiom sounded unperturbed.

I didn't know cataracts had been operated on so long ago. I stole a glance at my son who was busy counting his points. He was living in a golden age, indeed. Well, almost golden. There was still a little problem with communication. Mail was slow, and there were no telephones, telegrams, televisions, or tele-anythings to transmit news. Writing, talking, shouting, singing – these were the choices we had, or pigeons at a pinch. Birds were the quickest means of getting messages across. Birds were even dyed different colours, for quick, coded signals. Smoke signals and drums were used. In some places, there were strategically placed whistlers who could pass along a complicated message almost as fast as the ancient telegrams. But the whistlers lived in a valley in the south-west of Gaul, and their whistles were a secret the tribes of that region guarded carefully.

When mail came, we all wanted to see it. I knew Alexander, however. He needed to be alone with his. When he finished, he would tell us everything he thought we needed to know in a long, drawn-out ritual.

He rarely let me look at the letters he received; mostly they were kept in a small, elegant, ebony box. It didn't lock, but I would never have dreamed of opening it and reading his mail.

I was chafing because I wanted to hear about my children. The rest of the politics in the world at that time didn't interest me, beyond what directly influenced my life. Not so Alexander. He had to have news from everywhere. The people who wrote to him, Usse, Ptolemy, Artabazus, and Nearchus, for example, wrote to him in code. They were careful never to let on that Alexander was still alive. I had insisted on that point, and men, being what they are, happily invented a system of passwords and coded messages that took hours to figure out, and kept them busy. Alexander adored it, and I'm sure the others did too. At any rate, Alexander managed to receive messages just about anywhere that we landed, be it by bird, boat, or chariot-express.

I wanted to know if any of the letters were from Ptolemy, and what he had to say about the children.

Of course, Alexander wasn't about to tell me right away. First, he'd make me wait until I was practically begging. Then he'd tease me; giving me titbits of information and making me guess the rest. It was his way of letting the news last as long as possible. He would draw out the whole thing until I lost my temper. I always swore I wouldn't get angry, and every time he'd goad me until I snapped. Well, not this time. I would be cool, calm, and dignified. I drew a brush through my hair and looked at Alexander out of the corner of my eyes as he walked into the room. He wore a preoccupied frown. Some news was not good.

Plexis glanced at his friend, but he knew him too well. 'What is it?' he asked, seriously.

Alexander opened his mouth, then shut it tightly. Mutely, he looked out the window at the gathering dusk. He didn't look at us. He stood, his back to us, and refused to answer when I asked what was the matter.

Plexis, Axiom, and I looked at each other. Usually, Alexander would share a funny anecdote, an important piece of information, or even a nugget of gossip, if only to whet our appetites. Then he would tease us, boyishly laughing at our interpretations. Plexis and Axiom loved to play along. Even Paul would join in, twisting the scraps of news into wild tales, to Alexander's hilarity. Only I would get impatient and cranky – to the men's delight, I'm sure.

We had been together for twelve years now, Alexander, Plexis, Axiom, and I; we knew each other well. For twelve years, we'd passed the time in harmony. Never, in twelve years, had Alexander turned his back on us and shut us out.

Plexis got to his feet, then went to Alexander. He didn't speak; he simply put his hand on Alexander's arm and stood next to him.

Axiom looked at me, picked up the pieces of the game we'd been playing, and left the room. Paul whispered that he was going to go bathe and left as well. I sat still, watching Plexis and Alexander standing motionless in front of the window. After a moment, I got awkwardly to my feet, smoothed my robe over my belly, and went to see Axiom. I caught a glimpse of Alexander's face as I left. Tears left streaks down his cheeks. His eyes were desolate. His shoulders were stiff; he didn't acknowledge Plexis's arm around him. I moved away quietly. If it had been bad news about the children, he would have told me. It was a private grief, one he had to face alone. I only hoped he wouldn't fall ill with his 'melancholy madness', because the only one who could treat that was Usse, and he was in Alexandria, three weeks away.

Chapter Thirteen

Three weeks! If I could have blown wind into the sails to make the boat go faster, I would have. I sat at the stern and stared at the billowing sails, as if my gaze could push the boat along.

I watched the blue water slide by the hull, white foam lacing the black wood. Dolphins danced in our wake, flying fish skipped across the waves, seagulls called loudly in the cerulean sky, and all this emphasized Alexander's sadness. The waves, the rise and fall of the ship, and the endless horizon evoked Alexander's admiral, his friend, his lover, and his confidant. The sea was Nearchus's kingdom.

Ptolemy's message had been news of Nearchus. Somewhere off the coast of Africa his boat had been set upon by pirates. Nearchus had been captured and assuredly killed.

That wasn't the only bad news Alexander had received. From Persia came news of Perdiccas' death. He'd been betrayed and killed by his own officers.

I didn't dare tell him the slaughter was far from over. Somehow, I'd always managed to dodge the matter. I couldn't tell him that the betrayals and treason would only intensify, accelerate, and finally end with the complete annihilation of Alexander's family and most of his friends.

Nearchus's death was a terrible blow to Plexis as well. Although he stayed with me because I was pregnant, I knew that part of him wished he'd gone with Nearchus. With Alexander and Plexis grieving for their friend, I felt helpless.

Luckily, Yovanix and Phaleria were around for company; otherwise, the three weeks we spent sailing would have been unbearable for me. Yovanix wanted to know everything about Alexandria, so Paul and I described the city. Phaleria was sure she was pregnant and, as it was her first child, asked me endless questions. It was a welcome diversion. I drew some sketches showing the baby in a woman's womb in the different stages of development. I told her what things to eat and what to avoid, and reassured her countless times a day that everything was normal and perfectly fine.

Demos, who'd lost his first wife in childbirth, was as nervous as Phaleria, and sacrificed nearly all our chickens to Hera.

I was nearing my eighth month of pregnancy. When I walked, I walked slowly. My appetite diminished, and I started to have trouble sleeping at night. Heartburn plagued me during this time. Axiom ground up some medicine and gave me the chalky stuff to swallow after my meals. I wasn't used to feeling poorly. Before, I'd always had lots of energy right up until the last week. I was worried, and went to see Axiom. He told me I was simply nervous. Vix concocted potions guaranteed to give me back my vitality and make the baby strong.

For three weeks I rested as much as my heartburn and nerves would let me. I tried to eat the various dishes Erati made to tempt me. I tried; I honestly did try. I played dice with Oppi and Paul, and admired the fish they caught. I spoke to Phaleria, doing the drawings, explaining the symptoms she was feeling, and soothing her fears. I also spoke to Demos, pointing out how natural it was to have children, and asked him to let Erati keep *some* chickens.

By the time we were nearly in Alexandria, I was feeling depressed. Alexander and Plexis had barely spoken to me for the entire trip. They hadn't spoken to anyone, really, they were quiet and distant, each alone with his own sorrow, but they had erected an invisible wall between them and me. I felt it keenly, and it broke my heart although I tried not to show it. I was also tired, so very tired of travelling. And looking into my future, I could only see more of the same. Alexander was doomed, like Odysseus, to be an eternal voyager. And how ironic it was, seeing that Odysseus had first to find Persephone before he could make his way back home.

Ptolemy had made Alexandria the capital of Egypt. And, as Alexander had remarked, it would make it very difficult for us to live there. I hadn't thought about that too much. I had been looking forward to going home. It was important for me. Perhaps my pregnancy made me more attached to that concept; perhaps I was simply tired of travelling. Twelve years of constant voyaging was taking its toll at last. However, we arrived to an atmosphere totally different from anything I was expecting.

For one thing, our house was no longer our home. Usse had been wounded when the druids came looking for Paul a year ago. He'd taken the children and fled, intending to take shelter with Ptolemy, who was living in Alexandria, having decided to make her the Capital. The king took the children and Usse into his court. Usse had a certain reputation as a doctor, and Ptolemy insisted he stay with him. Usse would have preferred to remain at home and work at the new hospital, which is what he had been doing. However, Ptolemy was persuasive. And besides, in those days you didn't say 'no' to a king.

Chirpa and Usse now lived in Ptolemy's palace with Brazza, who took care of Chiron and Cleopatra. Then Ptolemy had formally betrothed Cleopatra to his son. It was an interesting political move. Ptolemy didn't proclaim Cleopatra as Alexander's daughter. By promising his son to a nobody, Ptolemy was saying, 'I ally myself with no one, my kingdom suffices unto itself'. He was also covering his bases with his gods. Outsiders beware. However, for Ptolemy to be truly considered god-king, Alexander had to be dead. We would not be able to live in Alexandria. It was another keen sorrow for Alexander, who loved his first city. It was also a terrible chagrin for me; I'd loved our home on the hillside.

Ptolemy received us in secret. We filed into his chambers, hot, tired, and weary from three weeks at sea. He met our boat with a special guard and they escorted us straight to the palace.

Alexander, Plexis, and I stood in front of Ptolemy, and I don't know who was angriest with him. Alexander, because he'd taken over his beloved city and sent bad news by mail, Plexis, because he had made Usse his personal physician. Or me, because my children and Brazza were nowhere in sight, and I was dying to pee.

I was too dispirited and pregnant to think about scaring Ptolemy with a good goddess act. Those types of things take energy and a nice nosebleed. Instead I stood, head high and as haughty as I could manage, hoping that the robe I was wearing was clean, and wondering where I could pee. In that potted palm, or over there, in the corner; was that a potty or a spittoon?

I crossed my legs, gritted my teeth, and waited for Ptolemy to finish speaking to Alexander. They were talking quietly together. Plexis stood a little to the side and every now and then he'd interrupt. He had no fear of Ptolemy, and I sensed exasperation beneath the surface of his calm. Alexander appeared dejected. He had no energy. His shoulders slumped. I wanted Usse to come so that he could treat Alexander for his melancholy.

I sighed and peered at the pot in the corner. It was starting to look more and more like a toilet.

Finally, the meeting seemed over. Ptolemy had said his piece. Alexander had muttered something I didn't quite catch, and Plexis had started to say something. Then he had clenched his jaw and had taken my arm and led me to the antechamber where Axiom and Paul were waiting.

'Stay here,' he said. He wasn't cold or angry with me; he was polite, as if we were strangers.

I waited until he closed the door behind him. Then my face crumpled. I sat down on a very intricately carved bench and I said to Axiom, 'If you don't find me a chamber pot in three seconds I'm going to pee right on this chair.'

He gaped at me. Then he grabbed the large bowl of nuts on the table, tossed them to the ground, and put the bowl at my feet. 'Be my guest,' he said.

Axiom was kind enough to call a slave to empty the bowl before anyone came back in the anteroom and saw it. The slave also picked up the nuts, which was a pity, because I was really hoping Ptolemy would stride into the room, step on the nuts, and take a spectacular fall.

He didn't come into the room though. Plexis and Alexander came back looking exhausted. Plexis said to me kindly, 'Don't worry, the children are with Brazza. We'll see them tomorrow.'

I didn't protest. I was used to the convoluted protocol that surrounded every one of Ptolemy's moves. He'd always been enigmatic, and now he was king. Tomorrow I would see the children. I knew they were safe. Ptolemy's word was sacred.

We went to the villa on the hillside, which had not been lived in for nearly a year. The pool was green and scummy, the fountain dry. Food had spoiled in the pantry, and rats had gnawed on the precious wooden furniture. Dust lay thick on the tabletops, the counterpanes were frayed by the wind, and thieves had forced a window open and made off with anything that could be carried away.

We stared in dismay, wandering through the echoing, empty rooms. Axiom was the first to react. He took coins from Alexander's box and left the villa. He was going to get some food, I assumed. I sighed, picked up a broom, and started to sweep the kitchen.

While I picked up the mess, I asked Paul to find himself a bedroom and fix it up.

'What do you mean, "fix it up"?' he asked.

'Find sheets, make your bed, open a window and air out the room. I don't know; use your imagination. We'll have to do it quickly, it's already late afternoon and the nights are cool,' I said snappishly. Then I shook my head. 'I'm sorry, I didn't mean to yell. If you could find a broom somewhere and start to sweep the rooms, that would be helpful.'

Paul looked undecided, but then left me alone. I opened the grain bin and squeaked as a mouse skittered across it. Well, let that alone for now, I decided. The dishes were gone, the thieves had taken them, and what they didn't take they had smashed. I carefully picked up shards of pottery and put everything in an old keg. The fireplace was full of ashes; I swept it out and lugged the ashes outside. Then I took some wood and made a little fire in the kitchen to keep me company and to cook dinner. I did everything one-handed, and I didn't do too badly. I had become good at using my ivory hand for levering and carrying things. I could manoeuvre quite well, actually. I started to get a nice feeling of self-satisfaction.

I cleaned out the pantry, figuring Axiom would appreciate somewhere to put the food. Then I attacked the stone counters. They needed dusting and cleaning, so I went to the well and hauled a bucket of water to the top.

Of course, that's when I lost my own waters. They broke, soaking my robe. I stood there in shock, the bucket in my hands. 'Oh, please, tell me it's a dream,' I begged, to nobody in particular. Plexis and Alexander were somewhere in the house. I hadn't seen them since we'd arrived, and frankly, I hadn't wanted to. They had been distant to me, acting as if I were a shadow. I knew it was simply their grief, but it frightened me. I'd grown too accustomed to being beloved.

With that thought, my mouth twisted. During my depressing childhood, I'd been totally ignored. It had made me wary of emotions such as love and passion. Alexander had tamed me. He'd made me open my heart. Sometimes I felt raw, as if I were being whipped by things I'd never dealt with before – like sorrow or joy. It hurt, but it was proof that I could feel *something*. Now he was ignoring me, something he'd never done. And it was the worst feeling I'd ever had.

No, actually I was wrong. A searing contraction left me clinging to the side of the well. It was so sudden I had no time to prepare for it. I screamed. No, *that* was the worst feeling I'd ever had. It made the time Roxanne tried to poison me feel like a slight stomach ache.

The cramps faded as abruptly as they'd come. I pried my fingers from the stone and wiped my forehead with a shaky hand. I'd better start boiling water. And I'd better tell my husband and Plexis what was happening.

I carried the bucket to the house and poured it into a large kettle that the thieves had found too heavy to carry away. The kettle was attached to a chain that went over a pulley, which hoisted it over the fire without any effort. I set the water on to boil and went in search of clean sheets. If I knew anything about having babies, it was that the process tended to be long, sometimes painful, and always messy.

'What do you mean the baby's coming?' Alexander raised his head, a blank look on his face. He was sitting behind a massive desk – another thing too big to carry away – and he'd been studying a parchment. His face was half in deep shadow, half in light. It made him look mysterious.

'I mean, the baby is coming. I'm in labour, if you prefer it that way.' I bit my lip as a cramp twisted through me. I didn't like the feel of that pain, it seemed much too far back. Not like a contraction should feel. A tiny stab of worry made me frown. I had been concentrating on my body, so I didn't even notice when Alexander stood and came to my side. In a moment, he changed. From indifference to panic, I think, would describe it best.

'Plexis! Axiom!' His voice was high.

'Axiom left an hour or so ago, I think he went to the city for some food,' I said helpfully, trying to pull Alexander's hand off my arm. 'You're hurting me.'

'Sorry!' He let go and stepped back. Then he grabbed me again and bellowed for Plexis. 'It's too early,' he cried.

'I hope not,' I said.

Plexis came into the room. He was naked, his hair wet from the bath. He saw me.

I was watching his face closely, holding my breath. He looked at Alexander, then at me, and his face tightened. It was fear; at least I hope it was fear. 'What is it?' he asked.

I managed a weak grin. 'Don't worry, but please, go get Usse. I want him with me. Please?' I couldn't see his face any more; tears were blinding me. I didn't stop grinning though. I was so afraid that he would speak to me in that polite tone of voice again.

He didn't say anything, but that was fine. He came to me and he kissed me tenderly. 'I'm going to fetch Usse, and Chirpa, and Brazza, and the children. I promise, I'll bring them all back here.' His voice broke.

'First get dressed, and then get Usse!' Alexander tossed him a cloak and pushed him out the door. I stood in a small patch of yellow sunlight and felt its warmth for the first time in three weeks.

Paul had managed to find some sheets and I picked out a bed. It wasn't easy. I insisted on walking through the bedrooms and inspecting them. One had a broken window; that would never do. One was too cold and another too hot. One was too dark. I tried to explain to Alexander that it was important I felt good in a room, because I felt awful just then. The contractions were deep, tearing things that made me gasp. I wanted to walk as much as I could, letting gravity help the labour. When the pain was too sharp, I leaned against Alexander. He held me tightly. His hands were shaking almost as much as mine were. I think we both knew the labour was going to be hard. I was worried, but didn't want to think about it. The baby was coming, and that's what mattered.

We finally settled on what had been Plexis' room – a large, airy chamber adjacent to the kitchen and garden. Alexander left me alone long enough to sprint to the neighbour's house and beg for some honey, salt, and wine.

The honey was useful. At that time it was used as a balm, a sweetener, an antibiotic, for marinating, and for embalming, even. The salt was to put in boiling water, and to use as an antiseptic. The wine was to wash the baby, and to drink, of course.

I sat on the bed and tried to count the minutes between contractions. They seemed to have no pattern, coming at irregular intervals. When they did come, they were horrible. I felt wrung out and weak afterwards, trembling with nerves and pain. Alexander was white-faced and even more upset than I was.

'As soon as Axiom returns, why don't you go to the harbour and get my belongings from Phaleria's boat?' I said gently. 'Axiom should be back any minute now, and Plexis won't be too long. Take Paul with you and leave him there, please?'

He looked at me, his eyes huge. 'Is it going that badly?' he asked, his voice husky with fear.

'No, of course not,' I said, trying to put some certitude into my words. 'I'll be fine, as soon as Usse comes. But I don't want Paul to hear me if I scream.'

'He was with you on the boat,' he said. 'You hardly cried aloud then.'

'Every birth is different,' I said. 'He was younger too, and less impressionable. The house is too big and empty; he'll be frightened. I want to be able to relax and only think about myself for a while. Please? I know I'm being selfish, but it can't be helped.'

Alexander took my hand in his. 'I want to apologize for these past weeks. I don't know what happened to me. Something within me changed, and I was helpless to prevent it.'

The tone of his voice told me nothing. 'Do you still care for me?' I whispered, staring at my hand.

His surprise was almost comic. 'Did you ever doubt it?' he asked.

I blinked, and tears slid down my cheeks. 'You know I did,' I said sadly.

'You're right. I did know. I'm sorry.'

'You wanted to punish me, somehow. But I'm not responsible for what happened. And I'm not your mother.'

His hand tightened on mine. He started to say something, then thought better of it. Instead, he kissed me. It was more appropriate than anything he could have said to me. It almost took my mind off my cramps. He waited until Axiom returned, then he left, taking Paul and swearing he'd be back as soon as possible.

When I could, I got up and walked around the room, leaning on the windowsill to gaze at the last of the sunset. Axiom stored the food away, finished cleaning the kitchen, and took over boiling water and finding clean sheets for me. He was relieved when I told him Plexis had gone to fetch Usse.

'Would you like some tea?' he asked me.

'If it's the tea that Vix made, I'd love some,' I said, wincing as a cramp hit again. Vix knew how to brew a potion that would take most suffering away. Unfortunately, it wasn't for childbirth pain. The contraction came in a wave this time, cresting right over and submerging me. Axiom held onto my shoulders. He was strong, but I missed Alexander's strength and I needed Usse's help.

The sky was orange and the shadows were deep when Usse came to the house.

I burst into tears and flung my arms around him. He held me, then backed away to get a good look at me.

'How is it going?' he asked.

I shook my head. 'Not good. The baby hadn't descended when the pains started.'

He glanced at Plexis. 'I'll need my medical supplies,' he said. 'Will you get them for me? I left them in the atrium.'

Plexis acquiesced, but before he left, he kissed me again.

Usse helped me lie down. Then he examined me, his face a study in concentration. While he probed and prodded, he asked questions about our voyage, and I was glad to answer, to keep my mind off the labour. He looked at my missing hand. I told him how I'd lost it. He admired the work Demos had done. His face was drawn, though, and his eyes sorrowful.

Finally he sat back and said, 'The babe is head down, but facing backwards.'

'What does that mean?' I asked.

'It means that it will take longer. But the baby's head is engaged in the birth passage, so we must be patient.' Usse wiped his hands on a clean towel. Then he moved the low stool near my pillow. 'It means we have more time to talk,' he said, with a smile.

'You don't fool me, you know,' I said, taking his hand in mine. 'You're worried. So, talk. Tell me about Chirpa, Brazza, Chiron and Cleopatra. Are they well?'

'They are. Chirpa blessed me with a child three months ago. We named him Abraham.'

'Congratulations,' I said.

'Your children are both very well. Chiron has an exceptionally quick mind. He drives his tutors crazy asking questions all day long. He grows tall and longs to see you again. Cleopatra promises to be as beautiful as her mother,' he said with a smile.

I grinned, then blanched as another wave of pain washed over me. When it finished, I was drained. 'I don't think I'll be able to last,' I said weakly.

'Drink some of this,' he said, giving me a sweetish beverage.

I drank thirstily, then sighed. 'I do feel better.'

'You're dehydrated. Have some more.'

'Tell me about Brazza, how is he?'

'He is happy when he is with the children. Now he looks after little Abraham as well, and Chirpa says she couldn't do without him. She is anxious to see you; she missed you very much. We all did,' he added.

'Oh.' I blinked. I wasn't used to having people say they missed me. I looked at the mound my stomach made and sighed. 'I wish the baby would hurry. I missed everyone and long to see them.'

Plexis returned and wanted to sit with me, but I asked him to leave. He looked stunned, but Usse shot him a warning glance. He left, a troubled expression on his handsome face.

Usse stayed with me during my seemingly never-ending labour. The night passed, morning came and the sun climbed across the sky. Still the pains came, wrenching and excruciating, leaving me exhausted. I tried to walk whenever I could. My back hurt terribly, but soon even sitting was too great an effort. I felt my strength draining from me. When evening came again, I lay on the bed and stared out the window. Everything was painful – noises, and even the fading light, seemed cut out of crystal. I couldn't move my arms or legs. Even my heartbeat hurt. The contractions were a giant hand now, which gripped me and shook me until I was rattling.

Plexis and Alexander were waiting outside. Usse told them that I needed to be alone. They didn't understand, and poked their heads into the room at least three times an hour. Finally Usse, out of exasperation and real worry for me, told them to go away. He remained beside me and gave me a cool cloth to bite, and smoothed my hair from my hot forehead. Every now and then, he'd give me a sip of some potion he'd made to keep up my strength. However, it was slipping away. The labour was too long, too arduous, and I was in no shape to fight. A year of hard travel, the shock of losing my hand, and seeing Alexander almost die in of the Game of Phersu, had weakened me.

Usse tried everything, making drinks, massages, prayers, and finally, shaking his head sorrowfully, he told me he had to bring the baby out with birthing irons. He went in search of Alexander. He would need his strength.

I simply closed my eyes. Nothing would be worse, I thought. I was even looking forward to just dying and having done with all the fuss and pain.

The irons woke me up. I screamed then, shattering my voice.

The baby was born after a long time. Alexander held me tightly, so tightly I had bruises on my arms for days. Usse had to use the irons, as he'd done with Mary. My sweet Mary. I thought of her often during this childbirth. For some reason, I thought the baby would be born dead. It didn't seem possible that such a tiny creature could bear such horrendous pain, although Usse assured me that *I* was the only one in pain. The baby was fine.

When I heard the crying, it seemed to come from very far away. Then I emerged from the apathy that had gripped me and opened my eyes. 'Boy or girl?' I asked weakly.

'Boy,' said Usse, holding the squalling infant in his arms. 'And he's huge! No wonder it took so long, and no wonder you were in such pain. Look at the size of him. A veritable giant.' He let his breath out in a shuddering sigh. 'Please, Ashley, don't scare me like that again.'

I grinned. At least, I think I did. I don't remember anything clearly until about three days later.

Everyone was in the house then. Brazza, the children, Usse, Chirpa, and little Abraham were staying in the west wing. Phaleria and Demos, Plexis, Alexander, Axiom, and I were in the east wing. I was surrounded by friends and family, and I managed to get through the baby blues without any trouble.

My new son was a big baby, for those days. In my time, four kilos was considered normal. He was large-boned and fair; making me think he looked like my side of the family. My mother had been very tall, and my father had nearly topped one metre ninety in his youth. I'd only ever seen him bent over a cane though, and our family didn't believe in holo-photo albums. So I have no way of knowing for sure if Atlas – that's what we named him – took after my father or not. When he was fully grown, Atlas measured two metres tall. He towered over us, bringing to mind our dear friend Millis. He wore his straight, ash-blond hair in a long ponytail, and his eyes were glacial blue chips of ice. However, that was twenty years in the future. Right now, I was recuperating in my bed, my husband at my side, watching as Atlas suckled noisily.

He'd been so frightened when Usse came to get him, that now he hardly left me. Plexis had been terrified as well. He'd grasped Alexander's tunic, crying and begging him to forgive him. Alexander had not understood, until Plexis sobbed that he was sure that I was dying. Usse had gaped, then pried Plexis's hands off Alexander. He told Plexis to get drunk, and told Alexander to wash his hands and come quickly. Plexis took Usse at his word, and had the worst hangover I'd ever seen. When he came in to see the baby, he nearly vomited on me.

I was fully awake now. Before, I'd been floating in a sort of half-dream state, thankfully doped with some of Vix's magic potion. Now I was awake and extremely uncomfortable. I shifted in the bed and winced. Alexander took the baby from me and held him while I tried to find a comfortable position to sit.

'Can you tell me the good news, or are you going to make me beg?' I said, peeved. 'If it's that good, would you be so kind as to tell me? You've been beaming at me for a half an hour now, and I know it's not because of the baby.'

Alexander looked startled, then, to my surprise, started to weep. I froze, my hand beneath my hip. 'What is it?' I asked, worried.

'It's a strange bit of news, and I don't know how to explain it,' he said, wiping his face with the baby's blanket.

'Start with the beginning.'

He sat down and put the baby in his cradle. 'Usse was with Ptolemy when the Nubian messenger came with Nearchus's diary. He waited until the man left. Then he followed him into the street and spoke with him. It seems that Nearchus may still be alive. The Nubian said that a man was sold by the pirates and taken inland by natives. He thinks that the man was Nearchus, because he was described as having "a helmet of golden hair". Usse believes that he was sold to work in the salt mines.'

'The salt mines?'

'I have to rescue him,' said Alexander, taking my hand in his.

'Why didn't Usse tell you before?'

Two red spots appeared on Alexander's cheeks. 'I think he was angry with me for not taking better care of you,' he said.

'Oh.' I hid a grin. 'I'm sorry.'

'No, I deserved it.' He sat on the side of the bed and touched my face. 'I'm a fool.'

'It's good news then, isn't it? Do you think he's still alive?' I smiled at my husband. 'You do, don't you?'

'I do, and I want to save him.'

'Fine, good idea. Where is the salt mine?'

'Draw me Africa,' he ordered, grabbing parchment and a pen from his desk. I complied, and he pointed to a spot not far from modern-day Algeria. 'He was attacked by pirates there. Then the next time he was seen, he was sold here,' and he pointed to a spot not far from Carthage.

'We were so close to him, then,' I said, shaking my head in wonder.

'The salt mines are near a great lake, in the land of the Nubians. That is where the messenger thinks he was being taken.'

'Poor Nearchus,' I said, and tears filled my eyes. 'Of course we have to go rescue him. As soon as I can move we'll leave.'

'No.' Alexander's expression was strange, and I'd thought I'd seen them all.

'What is it?' I asked, my heart suddenly thumping very hard.

'No, I can't take you with me. It's too dangerous.'

I sat up straighter now, a hot flush on my cheeks.

'Dangerous? You dragged me halfway around the world, into battle, through deserts, across mountains, and to a place called the 'Land of the Eaters of the Dead'. What could be more dangerous?'

'You have a new baby. You need to rest,' he said firmly.

'I can rest on a boat, or on a litter,' I cried. 'Please,' I said, starting to shake.

'No, you're too weak.'

'Don't be silly. Have you been listening to Plexis?'

'You nearly died,' he said quietly.

'I did not, who told you that?'

'Usse.' He scowled. 'You can't move right away, it will kill you.'

I felt as if I'd received a blow to the chest. Nothing he said made sense to me. 'It's not true,' I said. 'It's not true.' I repeated stubbornly. Angrily I hit his arm. 'Look at me when I speak to you! Why would Usse say that? It's not true!' My voice rose to a shriek and the baby woke up and began to cry. Alexander sat on the edge of my bed and he wouldn't meet my eyes. We sat there, the baby crying, until Usse came into the room to see what the matter was.

I turned to him. 'Usse, tell me the truth. Did I nearly die?'

'You did,' he said heavily.

I closed my eyes and tried to calm myself. 'How long was I asleep?'

'Three days.'

'What happened?'

'There was too much bleeding. You must stay in bed now until you are out of danger. I'm sorry. You will never have any more children.' Usse took my hand. 'My Lady,' he began carefully, 'If you travel now, it will surely kill you.'

I was very still. The baby stopped crying and went back to sleep. A fly buzzed lazily in the corner of the room. Dust floated in sparkling motes in the air. Alexander wouldn't look at me, and Usse's gaze never wavered.

I wiped the blood off my nose mechanically. My throat felt tight, but that was just raw emotion. I looked at Alexander and said, 'How long will you be gone?'

'I don't know.'

'Is Plexis going with you?'

'If he wants to.'

I nodded. 'Where will I stay?'

'You will stay here in our house. I will rescue Nearchus, and then I will come back and get you.'

'You sound so sure of yourself,' I whispered.

'I am. Ptolemy has given me gold to buy Nearchus's freedom. There will be no need to fight.

Chapter Fourteen

I was still in bed when they left. We knew Ptolemy was anxious to have us out of Alexandria. We told him we would leave, but not until Nearchus was safely back. Until then, I stayed in the house on the hill. Axiom, ever-faithful, went with Alexander and Plexis. Demos also insisted on accompanying them, much to Phaleria's annoyance.

Chirpa ran the household, but the work was done by slaves. I hated slavery and insisted the servants be freed. It was easily done, and the ex-slaves became our godchildren. Chirpa had been a slave, and it shocked me that she would buy one.

'How can you buy a person, Chirpa! You were once a slave. Doesn't it bother you?'

She thought about it, then nodded once, which meant 'no'. 'Slavery is part of life. The gods have decreed who shall be born free and who shall be a slave. They also decree who will be freed. We are simply fulfilling the gods' wishes. At any rate, we own no slaves any more. And our new god-daughter, Rahima, broke your favourite vase this morning when she dusted it.'

'I like Rahima better than the vase,' I said.

'Since Demos has gone with Alexander and Plexis, Phaleria has decided stay with us,' said Chirpa, deftly changing the subject.

Soon after Alexander left, I went to see Ptolemy. I had a few things to discuss with him.

I was unable to walk, therefore I hired a sumptuous litter to carry me to the palace, starting a fad that would last for centuries.

Ptolemy received me in the main throne room, which was a measure of his esteem for me. I frightened him, although he tried to hide the fact. To him, I was a goddess. I'd proved it by saving Alexander. Ptolemy had always been the most mystic of Alexander's generals, and the most ambitious. He was exquisitely polite. He hid his emotions behind that polished façade, fooling most mortals, I'm sure.

I was not like most mortals.

'My Lady,' he said, bowing to me.

We were alone, except for a deaf-mute. Ptolemy didn't want our conversation overheard. Good, I didn't want anyone to hear us either. 'I have come to thank you for keeping my children safe,' I said.

Ptolemy nodded gravely, flipping his wrist in a dismissive gesture.

'I have a message for you from my mother,' I said. Somehow, I kept a straight face when I said this. If Alexander had been with me, his jaw would have dropped. He hardly ever saw me drag out my alter ego. Ptolemy's jaw *did* drop. He gaped at me. Then he took a deep breath and asked me what it was.

'She told me to tell you that she approves of what you are doing. She will intercede on your behalf with Zeus.'

'On my behalf? With Zeus?' he said nervously. 'Why? For what reasons?'

'Because you have been instrumental in protecting those I care for. As long as I am happy, she is happy too,' I added ingeniously. 'I could not be happy without Usse, Chirpa, and my children, so I they are staying with me. You won't mind, will you?'

'Mind? No, why should I mind? If you wish Usse to stay with you, of course he may. Invite whomever you wish to your home. Please.' Ptolemy rarely babbled, but now he was practically tripping over his tongue in his haste to be agreeable. 'Iskander will not be long on his voyage, six months, no more. Three months to get there and three months back. Never fear for Nearchus, if he's alive, Iskander will buy his freedom.'

I nodded. Six months for me to rest and recuperate. Afterwards, I would be ready to travel. I smiled at Ptolemy and said, 'I thank you for everything you've done for us. I will wait here in Alexandria until Iskander returns. Then we will leave Egypt for good.'

Ptolemy gave a start at this. 'And your daughter?' he asked.

'She will return on her sixteenth birthday to meet your son. Their betrothal will be announced at that time. I give you my word,' I said, raising my chin.

'They've already met, my son and Cleopatra, that is. They play together in the palace, and I think they get along well.' Ptolemy said, trying for a placating smile.

I just looked at him gravely. I hadn't met his son, then a nine-year-old boy. He was with the royal family in their palace, and strictly off-limits to anyone. Even me.

Alexander and I had spoken very seriously about Cleopatra's marriage, and we'd concluded that a promise to Ptolemy was the best thing we could do for now. When she was sixteen, she would be old enough to decide if she truly wanted to marry his son or not. Whatever she decided, we would stand by her.

I had to make sure Ptolemy stayed on our side. If he wanted, he could make things very difficult for us. The more powerful he became, the easier it would be for him to eliminate those he considered his rivals. He only pretended to accept the fact that Alexander didn't want his kingdom. If he wanted his son to marry Cleopatra – and he did; he was convinced she was the direct descendent of a goddess – he had to make sure she stayed alive. But that didn't apply to her father, Alexander, or even to me. I knew that Ptolemy would kill me if he thought he could get away with it.

I would never trust Ptolemy, although he'd pledged his help to recover Nearchus. As long as Alexander was alive, Ptolemy would always be looking over his shoulder, waiting for him to claim his throne. There was only one way to get rid of a rival to the throne.

The six months we spent in Alexandria were idyllic. During this time, Phaleria gave birth to her son, a strong healthy baby. He would have no name until his father came back, so we called him Maponos, which was 'son' in Gaul.

As usual, the first nickname stuck, and we called him Maponos for ever after.

Nothing else of note happened. Usse and I planned how to save Alexander from Ptolemy. The boys grew close, riding and hunting together every day. Cleopatra didn't remember me; she was happiest with Brazza, Usse, and Chirpa. That broke my heart, but I could see she was loved. She was a beautiful child, and very sweet and docile. I had no idea where her gentle character came from. No one in my family or Alexander's were so good-natured. I decided she got it from Brazza, her adored godfather.

Alexander returned early one morning. I spotted him first. I overturned my chair in my haste to stand, then gave a glad cry and ran towards the five men riding slowly up the dusty road. Nearchus was alive – but very weak. Plexis and Demos rode on either side of him, propping him up. They had spent the last two months travelling through the desert, but the voyage, said Alexander, had been easy. They all had stories to tell of their adventure, and the next few days were spent listening to their tales of the salt mines and Nearchus's rescue.

'It wasn't a huge rescue,' Alexander said, obviously disappointed. 'It was more of a transaction. I paid the owner of the salt mine, and he gave me Nearchus.'

'You could have bargained,' put in Plexis. 'The owner of the mine said he was a terrible worker.'

'He did not!' said Nearchus, who laughed with us anyhow.

'Speaking of rescue,' said Usse. 'Ashley and I know that while Ptolemy is trying to pass himself off as a god-king, he can't allow to Alexander to live.'

Alexander looked startled, then his face settled in grim lines. 'I had thought of that,' he said. 'I don't know how to convince him I never want to rule again.'

'Ashley has a plan,' said Usse.

'Oh, no. Famous last words,' said Plexis. 'The last time Ashley planned something, we saved a boy from sacrifice, set fire to the sea, and got chased by Carthage's navy.'

'I don't know why *you're* complaining,' said Alexander. '*I'm* the one that nearly got killed. What could possibly be worse?'

Usse coughed. 'This time, you have to die,' he said.

After that discussion, things moved quickly. We put our plan into action right away. Demos and Phaleria left the house with their son. They wanted to ready the boat. Yovanix and the crew had been staying there, but Demos needed to buy supplies and Phaleria wanted to make sure the dragon boat was seaworthy.

We packed what we needed, then sent word to Ptolemy that Alexander had contracted a fever. Usse had left supplies at the palace, so he wrote asking Ptolemy to send them quickly. When Ptolemy sent his messenger to us, Alexander feigned illness. We carried him to the atrium on a litter, and made sure that the messenger saw he was seriously ill. Then, a few days later, we sent Ptolemy news of Alexander's death. Knowing that the king would not believe the news, Usse and Vix concocted a potion that made it appear as if Alexander were dead. We wrapped ourselves in mourning cloaks and cut off our hair.

Axiom and I stripped Alexander and washed him in an herbal bath that gave his skin a curious grey-green cast. With my makeup, I made deep shadows around his eyes and mouth. He looked so horrible Chiron burst into tears when he saw him. Then Alexander stretched out on a litter while we sewed him into a linen shroud.

'We're just going to sew it closed to your waist. Ptolemy has to be able to see that it's you. After, we'll close it all the way.' Axiom tied a knot in his thread and frowned. 'Don't move, you'll rip the stitches.'

'I hate not being able to move about,' Alexander complained, trying to get comfortable on the narrow litter. 'This shroud is scratchy.'

I patted his hand. 'It won't be for long. The worst part is going to be drinking Usse's potion, not getting wrapped in a linen shroud.'

'Promise me you won't be too sad. You only have to mourn for a few years – then maybe you can remarry, that is, if you can find someone who could ever replace me.'

'Ha, ha.' I stuck my tongue at him. 'I think it must be time to drink now. Ptolemy will arrive soon, and you have to be unconscious.'

'You weren't joking,' he said, gasping as he drank the bitter liquid. 'It tastes like camel piss!'

'As if you ever drank *that*,' I said. I waited until his eyelids closed, then went to get Usse. 'He's asleep. I have to go get dressed and get everyone into position. Are you sure he'll be all right? He looked deathly,' I said, worried in spite of my confidence in Usse.

'He will appear as if dead, but don't worry.' Usse glanced out the window. 'The sun sets. I will tell Axiom to ready the funeral pyre.'

'Will Ptolemy wonder at the haste?' I asked. 'Will he suspect trickery?'

Usse shook his head. 'No, it is hot out, and bodies will spoil quickly in the heat. Also, I think he will be too relieved to be rid of Alexander to question anything. When someone wishes something, it is easier for him to believe his wish has come to pass.'

I shuddered, but everything went as planned.

Ptolemy came to the funeral. He examined Alexander before we sewed him in the shroud, touching his face and his chest, but Usse's potion had done its work and Alexander was cold and still. Ptolemy also insisted that he help place Alexander's body onto the funeral pyre. Usse had been ready for that as well. In a trick worthy of a great magician, he swapped bodies. Remembering what Olympias and Sis had done, I rubbed ashes all over myself and threw myself on the ground, then I tore at my clothes, bared my breasts, and writhed and wailed, distracting Ptolemy so that Demos and Vix could lift Alexander off the pyre and hoist the cadaver Usse had taken from the hospital morgue onto the oil-soaked wood. It was done in a moment.

When I saw Axiom raise the torch, I stopped and made as if to throw myself on the funeral pyre. 'Not without me!' I screamed.

'No! Please!' Paul and Chiron grabbed my arms. We had rehearsed for the show, and the boys didn't forget their lines.

'Please, Mother, stay with us,' Paul wailed. 'Without Father, we need you! Who will take us to the Sacred Valley of Nysa if you die too?'

Chiron, already overwrought and emotional, burst into hysterical sobs. 'No, Mother, no! I won't let you. If you die, I will too. We'll all go with Father!'

I pretended to swoon, and Plexis carried me into the house and lay me on a couch near the open window so we could see the proceedings. Paul and Chiron stood in front of the fire, watching as the corpse burned.

We needed to distract Ptolemy. 'Oh, Plexis, what would I do without you?' I said loudly. Ptolemy turned and saw Plexis soothing me with a passionate kiss – from his raised eyebrows I could tell he hadn't imagined how close we were. And then Rahima managed to drop another vase, this one full of flowers and water, so that it smashed on the floor. Chirpa made a great fuss about that. What really captured Ptolemy's attention, though, was Nearchus stalking about wailing, his hair cut short and ashes smeared on his face. With all the goings-on, Ptolemy never noticed the strange pile of sheets and laundry Usse transported in the handcart as he quickly removed Alexander from the courtyard.

'I'm sorry I ever thought Nearchus was a bad actor,' I murmured into Plexis's ear.

Plexis caught Ptolemy staring at us and he faked a huge sob. 'I don't think I can live without him,' he cried, burying

226

his face in my bosom. 'Let me comfort you some more, Ashley. You look distraught.'

'If you don't stop fondling me, Ptolemy is going to call for wedding banns.' I slapped his hand away. 'And the children are right outside.'

'Can't help it. You make the most ravishing widow,' he chuckled.

'If you blow this, Ptolemy will make sure I am a *real* widow,' I said sternly.

'The fire will last all night. How are we going to keep this up?' Plexis sighed and got to his feet. Let us start the funeral feast. Maybe we can get Ptolemy so drunk he'll fall asleep, then we can all get some rest.'

The feast went smoothly – except for Rahima, who was not meant to be a serving girl. Finally, Chirpa sent her to the kitchen to help clean the dishes. We winced whenever we heard another dish breaking.

After the funeral feast, and after the fire had died down, Ptolemy took the ashes and had them interred in a massive tomb he'd built near his palace.

We left Alexandria right after the funeral. The most bitter part of the bargain was that I had to leave Cleopatra behind. Ptolemy believed Alexander was dead, and he thought I was returning to the Sacred Valley in Nysa. He didn't trust me to bring Cleopatra back. Brazza stayed with her, and Usse and Chirpa. I knew she'd be surrounded by people who loved her, but I was shattered with grief.

'We will be back,' Alexander said, embracing me. 'We will visit whenever we can.'

'I know. And she will be happy. But Alex, I'm so sad. I can't believe we're leaving her behind.'

'And Usse and Chirpa and Brazza. She will stay in the house on the hill, and she will have a wonderful childhood,' said Alex. 'Just think, she will have a normal life!'

I laughed then, and let him kiss my tears away.

My life had been one long voyage – through time, and now, across the known world. But Alexander was with me. And so was Plexis, and my sons, and my friends. My heartache would ease. As the boat slipped through the green water, I looked at the man who would become a legend, and he smiled at me.

After Egypt, we travelled throughout the kingdom, going to Athens, Rhodes, Tyre, and Iberia. We never went back to India, although Alexander often dreamed of that, and we never ventured to Macedonia or Babylon – because of the war, and the ghosts. Alexander never spoke of them, but he was haunted all his life. The ghost of his father was the most terrifying, but the shades of his mother, wives, and children would often wake him in the middle of the night, and he would light a lantern and sit until dawn.

Mostly, we travelled with Demos and Phaleria. The dragon boat was swift, and we were glad to sail with good friends.

We did go back to Rome. Chiron, who was fascinated by Rome and all things Roman, lived there for many years with Scipio's family. He married a Roman woman and they had four children. We went often to visit, and no one ever recognized Alexander.

We made the trip to the great north a few times, even staying one whole winter. Alexander was always invigorated by the cold, while Plexis shivered and complained. Paul chose to live there. His children sailed the seas on dragon boats, and luckily, none of them seemed to inherit Alexander's seasickness.

Yovanix voyaged with us for a while, then married a girl he met in Britain, where he settled and lived out his long life. We spent a few years there with him, and we met Myrddin again.

Atlas, the tallest and gentlest of my children, stayed with us until he married. Then, with his Celtic wife Mara, he left towards India. The stories he'd heard about the Sacred Valley of Nysa and India had always fascinated him. He wrote us hundreds of letters, for he loved mail almost as much as Alexander. He even travelled to China, and part of his family settled in the land of the Moguls. His letters were always a cause for celebration.

After Alexander saved Nearchus from the salt mines, he stayed with us while he recovered his health. Then his wanderlust took hold again, and he made a three-year voyage around the coast of Africa. He was the second man in history to make the journey. He published his notes and the book was a great success, one of the most popular ones in the great library in Alexandria. After, he went back to Crete. We heard from him for a few years, but then the letters stopped.

When the children were settled, we decided to go south. Alexander wanted to visit Africa. Nearchus had whetted his appetite with his fabulous stories. Therefore, we sailed down the Nile to the land of the Nubians, where Plexis was thrilled to see herds of striped horses, and Alexander cried with joy to see wild elephants.

Brazza stayed with his beloved Cleopatra. She grew up in the house on the hill and had a wonderful childhood. She was in love with Ptolemy's son, and her marriage was, on the whole, a happy one. However, she had to misfortune to lose two of her five children – her son to war, and her beloved daughter to an accident. But her eldest son would become Pharaoh, and so would his son, and so on, and so forth, until their dynasty ended with another Cleopatra, her great, great, ever so great-granddaughter, who fell in love with Mark Anthony.

I never told her the rest of the story. I only told her the first part, the part where she falls in love, and lives happily ever after. Some stories should never end, and I am well placed to know that.

There are several tombs purported to be of Alexander the Great. Only I know the real one. I will tell you this much; it is a simple tomb carved in stone. Inside are the relics of a legend. There is a gold cup in the shape of a winged lion, and a large round shield, supposedly magic, which once belonged to the great hero, Achilles. There is a long braid of pale hair, and many well-read letters in an ebony box, for he loved mail, and there is an ancient scroll that, when carefully unrolled, reveals a copy of *The Iliad*. He was never without it. He was afraid of the dark, so I put a lamp in his tomb to chase away the shadows.

He was buried alone, since he died before any of us. He was our sun, our god, and the reason we lived. Without him, the world appeared much darker, and smaller, somehow.

Before he died, we chose a place to settle. It is an enchanted land, pristine and tranquil. The Greeks call this land Aethiopia[1], and claim that the gods give great banquets here. They must be right. If there were anywhere on earth a god would go to have a banquet, it would be here.

Plexis, Axiom, and I live there now. We live near the coast, so mail comes regularly. We wait impatiently for news from the children. Our house is large, airy, and overlooks a silver lake. In the evenings, the animals go to the shore to drink. We sit on our veranda and watch as lions, zebras, cheetahs, and giraffes stride out of the dusk.

Plexis and I are together, and I am glad to have him near me. His quick wit, wry humour, and enthusiasm have never dimmed. When we lost Alexander, the bright sun set on our lives, but we live in a warm glow. We still hold hands at night beneath the gauzy mosquito netting. Our bodies still speak the silent language of love, and I need him so.

The sun is setting now. Soon, shadows will reach into the room and cool it for the evening. I smell woodsmoke; the cook has started dinner. In a moment, I will light the oil lamp, the blue glass one that swings gently from the ceiling.

---

[1] "Where south inclines westwards, the part of the world stretching farthest towards the sunset is Aethiopia (Ethiopia); this produces gold in abundance, and huge elephants, and all sorts of wild trees, and ebony, and the tallest and handsomest and longest-lived people." Herodotus, *The Histories*, (525 BC) English translation by A. D. Godley. Harvard University Press. 1920.

Beneath my feet, the Persian rug is soft and its colours are still jewel-like.

I hear Plexis laughing. He and Axiom are sharing some joke, or perhaps they are re-reading Paul's letter where he describes the way his son caught a salmon with his bare hands. Plexis will call for me soon; we always sit outside in the evening and watch the lions come to the edge of the lake to drink.

Now and then, I glance in the mirror. I have grown vain in my old age. Perhaps it is because Plexis hasn't lost his good looks. His hair is still dark, and his body is still straight and slim. I always had pale hair, though now it is white and short. I cut it off when Alexander died, and found it more practical to care for. Around my neck is the moonstone he gave me so long ago in Persepolis.

Alexander! The name is a whisper in the room, merging with the shadows and the cool, blue light cast by the lamp. There is still an echo of him; an echo that lasted for three thousand years. Sometimes I can almost feel him standing next to me.

I'm not afraid to die. In a way, I almost look forward to it. For one thing, I shall be buried next to Alexander, and there is a place for Plexis, and for Axiom in the tomb as well. We even joke about it. For you see, how can I be afraid of death? In three thousand years, I will be born again. I will win a prestigious award and be chosen to interview a legend. In three thousand years, I will return to Alexander, and the story will go on. The story will never end. I am looking forward to meeting Alexander again.

About the Author

Jennifer Macaire is an American living in France.

She likes to read, eat chocolate, and plays a mean game of golf. She grew up in upstate New York, Samoa, and the Virgin Islands. She graduated from St Peter and Paul High School in St Thomas and moved to NYC where she modelled for five years for Elite. She went to France and met her husband at the polo club.

All that is true. But she mostly likes to make up stories.

Á

Proudly published by Accent Press

www.accentpress.co.uk

9 781786 154583